FORGOTTEN EVIL

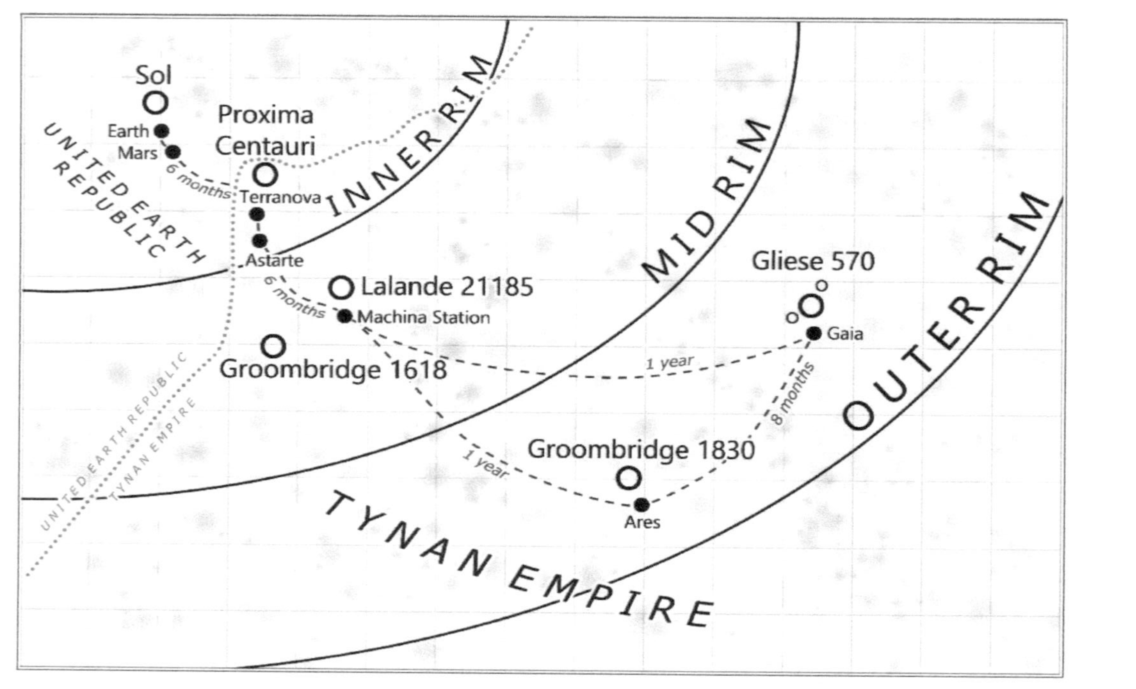

Sol
Earth
Mars
6 months
Proxima
Centauri
Terranova
Astarte
6 months
UNITED EARTH
REPUBLIC
INNER RIM
Lalande 21185
Machina Station
Groombridge 1618
MID RIM
Gliese 570
Gaia
1 year
8 months
OUTER RIM
1 year
Groombridge 1830
Ares
TYNAN EMPIRE
UNITED EARTH REPUBLIC
TYNAN EMPIRE

BOOK 1 | THE FORGOTTEN SAGA

FORGOTTEN EVIL

Quill Holland

ScorPress Publishing

Content Warning:
Forgotten Evil is intended for mature audiences and includes scenes with sexual material, violence, and offensive language which some readers may find distressing.

ISBN: 978-0-473-59733-7 (Paperback)
ISBN: 978-0-473-59734-4 (Epub)
ISBN: 978-0-473-59735-1 (Kindle)
ISBN: 978-0-473-59736-8 (PDF)

Cover design by Cover Creator UK
Map design by Dewi Hargreaves
Editing by CA Proofing

The ScorPress logo is a trademark of ScorPress Publishing Limited.

Published by ScorPress Publishing, New Zealand.
www.scorpress.pub

"In each of us, two natures are at war – the good and the evil. All our lives the fight goes on between them, and one of them must conquer. But in our own hands lies the power to choose – what we want most to be we are."

– Robert Louis Stevenson

Contents

Title Page
Copyright
Dedication
Epigraph
Prologue: The Arrival of a Stranger   1
Chapter 1: Happy Discovery Day!   3
Chapter 2: The Soul Harvest   14
Chapter 3: The Place Between Worlds   24
Chapter 4: A Shift in the Wind   35
Chapter 5: Home of War and Sex   44
Chapter 6: "Where Do You Think You're Going?"   53
Chapter 7: "You Know Me?"   57
Chapter 8: A Tale of Two Minds   65
Chapter 9: Reflection   76
Chapter 10: Manhunt   87
Chapter 11: The Puppet Master   96
Chapter 12: Planning is Essential   108
Chapter 13: Mass Conversion   116
Chapter 14: All Routes Lead to Home   125
Chapter 15: An Evil ... Forgotten   135
Epilogue: Something Wicked This Way Comes   145
Acknowledgements
Also by Quill Holland
About the Author

Prologue
The Arrival of a Stranger
2144, Common Era – Planet Gaia, Outer Rim, Tynan Empire

The arrival of a stranger was seldom a good thing, particularly in the Outer Rim. Bad things happened when strangers arrived, things like Soul Harvests or piracy. A farming couple entertained these thoughts as they stood over the stranger they'd found lying unconscious at the river's edge. But perhaps he wasn't a stranger to this planet, only to them. The farmer lifted the man, carrying him all the way to the planet's only medical centre. As the stranger drifted in and out of consciousness, the couple waited anxiously to discover who it was they'd found.

At long last, the doors to the room slid open as the assigned doctor entered.

"And?" asked the farmer. "Who is he? Where is he from?"

"That I cannot say. I know he's not a citizen of Gaia, and I checked if he was from Ares, but he isn't."

"So he's a pirate?"

"I don't think so. The full-body scans suggest that he's about thirty-three standard years old, in good physical condition – probably had an easy life. They also show that he's got severe post-traumatic dissociative amnesia because of extensive, unnatural neural trauma. This man's mind has been artificially tampered with and forcefully modified."

"And that doesn't make him a pirate?" the farmer inquired, derision filling his tone.

"We're not graced with the technology to perform such operations here in the Outer Rim, nor the Mid Rim for that matter."

The doctor paused, carefully thinking about how to phrase his following words.

"Therefore, I think it fair to surmise that he has come from the Inner Rim, and that is the domain of both the United Earth Republic and the core of the Tynan Empire – piracy doesn't flourish there."

"So, what does all of this mean?" implored the farmer's wife. "What will happen to him?"

"I am no fortune teller, but if I were to make an educated guess, I would say that this man is largely going to be a blank slate. He'll need to be cared for and supported as he forms a new identity."

The doctor watched as the couple exchanged a glance before checking his notes. "If I'm not mistaken, you are childless?" he queried.

"We had a daughter!" the farmer snapped.

"Livietta. She died five years ago," his wife added quietly.

"My condolences. Perhaps then, you could care for this man. I realise he is not a child, but he could become a strong set of farm hands in return for his board and lodgings."

The couple exchanged another glance.

"But he is a stranger!" the farmer disputed. "Bad things happen when strangers arrive!"

"This man is a stranger to himself! Trauma like his doesn't leave you knowing who you are. He'll need guidance, support: both of which I think you can offer him."

"And if bad things happen?"

"Then we'll send him to Ares – let the Empire's grunts deal with him."

With a final glance and a nod, the couple agreed.

"Fine ... we'll take him."

Chapter 1
Happy Discovery Day!

2146, Common Era – Planet Gaia, Outer Rim, Tynan Empire

They say that dreams are built from your memories, constructed out of long-term memories of the self or specific memories from significant events.

The only thing I ever dreamed about was an ocean of darkness. There was always the tiniest sliver of the moon, like a crack of light in an otherwise black sky, illuminating a horrifying truth – that I was alone, floating in an endless sea that stretched to the very edge of the horizon.

The water would start calm, but the longer I slept, the rougher it became until it had transformed into a thunderous storm. Waves as high as buildings would crash down upon me, plunging me to the depths where I would tumble about in the angry currents. Each time I would struggle to the surface, abating my fear as I gulped a lungful of air.

Again and again the cycle would repeat, sapping my strength until I had none left. That was when the biggest waves would come, ramming into me with immeasurable force. As I sank beneath the surface, I'd hold on to my last breath of air for as long as I could. But when the urge to breathe took over, I'd trade oxygen for salt water and awaken to a now-familiar voice.

"Drown!" it would hiss inside my head.

The doctor had called it a "side effect", nothing more than a consequence of the brain trauma. Yet, night after night, this was my reality. How long were trauma side effects supposed to last? As I lay in bed, sweaty and panicked, still reeling from the fear, I could only wonder why was this happening? What did it mean?

Why was I a thirty-five-year-old man with only two years of memory? As the sunlight began to creep through the curtains, I knew that the questions would have to wait until tomorrow. Just like they did every day.

❦

Walking into the kitchen, my parents greeted me in unison, "Happy Discovery Day!"

"What …?" I managed to mumble around a yawn.

"Happy Discovery Day!" my mother repeated. "Had you forgotten?"

Oh yes, I thought, remembering what day it was: the second anniversary of my discovery.

"I hadn't forgotten," I replied, sitting at the table. "I was hoping to remember, as always."

"Oh, my darling!" Mother exclaimed as she placed my breakfast before me. She placed a hand on my shoulder and squeezed, smiling down at me. "I know you want to remember, but the doctor did say that given the lack of any recollection these last few years, it's highly likely your memory won't ever return."

I knew she meant well, but she had a way of speaking down to me at times, as if I were a child.

"I know, Mother. I was there, remember?"

For a moment, her eyes became distant, as if she were struggling to recall the moment of which she had just spoken. "Oh yes, of course you were!" she said with a smile.

"She condescends …"

Not now, I thought, trying to suppress the dark voice inside. Refocusing, I realised my mother was still speaking to me.

"… of course, maybe I'm the one who needs to remember! The amount of things I forget, isn't that right, darling?"

"Mother, I don't want to talk about this right now."

"Why not?" she asked, her expression souring. "It's your Discovery Day, after all!"

"She doesn't listen …"

"Mother … please."

"Honey, let's talk about something else," Father interjected, motioning for her to sit down.

"Well, he's not going to remember if we never talk about his past, is he?" she argued.

"Honey …"

"Tell her …"

"Mother …"

"Don't honey me. Why do you always take his side?"

"Tell her!"

"Silence!" I yelled, leaping to my feet, the darkness taking control at that moment.

My mother moved backwards, cowering before me.

"Boy!" my father hollered. "Sit down!"

As quickly as it'd come, the darkness receded, and I collapsed back onto my seat. I looked at my mother, absorbing the look of fear her face still bore.

"I … I'm … I'm sorry, Mother." I stammered.

She scurried out of the room without a word, leaving me to face my father.

With a sigh, he leaned forward. "Son … you've got to remember the wolves."

"I know, Father … I know."

"I know you do, son. But every time the darkness arises, it's my job to refocus you. To remind you of which wolf to feed."

I nodded. My father was very good at maintaining perspective.

Yet viewpoints were relative. My perspective was formed from thirty-three blank and empty years and two that were full and vivid.

"Don't worry. Your mother will come right. Just give her time."

"I know," I mumbled, eyeing up my breakfast and finding myself uninterested in eating.

"Would you go into town for me please, son?" my father asked, pushing his chair back and standing.

"Yeah, of course."

"Great. I'll give you a list of things we need," he said, taking his dishes to the sink. Pausing as he placed them down, he looked back at me. "Best you eat up. Don't want the right wolf going hungry, aye?"

"Sure," I said, picking up my utensils.

"Oh, and one more thing."

I looked back at my father. "Yeah?"

"Whilst you're there, buy something for yourself, okay?"

"Sure thing. Thanks."

After my father left, I took my breakfast to the kitchen. A picture of Livietta sitting on the counter caught my eye. It was times like these when the illusion broke down and I remembered that I was the changeling – the substitute for a child taken. They never spoke about her, who took her or how she'd died – I suspected they didn't even know the whole truth. The hole in their lives that I filled was a hole that I did a poor job of filling. It mostly worked, except for the moments when it didn't.

❦

The EV glided along the road, sweeping through each corner and soaring down each straight. I'd often wondered what it would be like to drive a classic car.

The planetary archives contained many records detailing a time when people drove vehicles.

Not on Gaia, mind you, but on the motherland: Earth. The word resonated within. The doctor believed that I might've come from the Inner Rim, and the thought that I had been to and probably lived on other worlds was tantalising. If my dreams were based on forgotten memories of an ocean, there was credence to this idea. Gaia only had one sea, and I'd never been there. But Earth, Mars, and Terranova all had several oceans.

The feeling of deceleration broke me away from my thoughts. "Vehicle – why are you slowing?"

"Obstruction ahead. Please clear it to proceed," the EV replied as it came to a stop.

"Open the doors."

Natural light flooded into the interior as the doors silently slid apart. Grabbing onto a handle, I pulled myself out and stepped onto the road. Glancing around, I discovered the source of the obstruction: A lone figure standing in the middle of the road.

"'Alt! Goes no further, ya 'ear! This be a stickup, innit?" the figure called out.

"But sweet robber, I have nothing of value upon myself to give to thee!"

"Now, don't youse be gettin' clever wit' me! I 'ears you've got the best kisses in the land! And I've come t' steal one!"

"Well, I couldn't comment on such claims – I kiss too few people to know the quality of mine." I replied, trying not to smile.

"But, if you insist, I will let you steal a kiss, and in exchange, you let me continue on my way!".

The lone assailant laughed, breaking her well-crafted character "Safe passage is worth at least two kisses, maybe even three! It depends on how well you kiss."

I smiled as I watched her walk over to me. I held out my arms, and she walked straight into them, grabbing my face and pulling it towards her own. Her lips met mine, exchanging a soft and familiar greeting. One kiss became two, and then a third; each time our lips met, our kisses deepened further. I gripped her body tighter, pulling it as close as was physically possible. With a final lingering touch of our lips, she pulled back and looked at me with a beaming smile.

"That was … sensational. I might have to steal kisses from you more often."

"Oh, Amorina – where would I be without you?"

"You'd probably be in town by now," Amorina replied.

Laughter rolled from me, releasing any lingering tension from the morning. Amorina grinned and pulled my head back down, silencing me with another passionate kiss.

When our lips parted, I cupped her cheek in my palm. "Would you like to join me? We can continue this robbery on the way into town."

"I would like that very much, but only if we take a detour first."

"Consider it done!"

❦

As I stared at the pile of discarded clothing, I mused over how the detour had gone. As it turned out, Amorina's surprise was a picnic set up in "our place" – a tree grove sheltered from the elements, hidden from the world, just a short walk from the road – our little slice of paradise. My parents never questioned why the trips to town took as long as they did, but I was sure they knew why.

"Whatcha thinkin' about, sexy?"

Breaking away from my thoughts, I turned to look at Amorina, tracing my eyes over the curves of her body until I arrived back at her face. "How perfect this place is and how sensational you are."

The corners of her mouth curved into a coy smile. "Not too bad for a Discovery Day present then?"

"That was the biggest understatement ever! You've made today … mind-blowing!"

"I should hope so!" she replied, leaning in for a kiss.

"She distracts us …"

Her lips skimmed my cheek as I jerked back from the sudden presence of the darkness.

"And yet …" she said, pulling back, "you're still distracted. And not by me, unfortunately."

"I'm sorry …"

"Never apologise!"

"I don't mean to be."

Amorina nodded. "I know. Is it the voice again?"

"Yes," I sighed. "I snapped at Mother this morning. I didn't hurt her … just left her scared, was all."

"Lie back for me."

I obliged and Amorina moved closer, pressing her body against mine as she snuggled into me. Partially draped over my chest, she reached up with one hand and pushed back my hair. Her thumb traced along the now exposed scar that circled my head.

"I assume you haven't remembered anything new?"

"Of course not! I haven't remembered anything for two years – why would it change now?"

"I don't know, but it never hurts to check. I just … I get frustrated, like I know you do, with not knowing – I wish we knew the story behind this scar. How you got it, who gave it to you."

"I know …"

"The way it goes around your whole head … like someone pulled the top of your skull off."

"She doesn't know …"

"It has to be connected to your memory, right? It has to be!"

"Silence her!"

"Amorina, please … we need to stop talking about this. Please!"

"Okay."

"Coward …"

"Thank you."

"Yeah, no worries," Amorina said, rolling off me, an awkward silence filling the space between us.

"Listen, thank you for everything today. The picnic, the conversation, the sex." I wiggled my eyebrows at her, drawing a small smile from her. "It means a lot."

"It's my pleasure, sexy! You know I love you, right?"

"I do. And you know that I love you more than anything else in this world?"

"I do!" Amorina said as she leaned in for another kiss.

This time I met her and took control, deepening it until we were both gasping for breath.

As she pulled away, her smile had deepened, and her eyes shone. "As much as I want to go another round with you, we should get to town before your parents start to question why the trip takes so long!"

※ ＼ ♥ ／ ※

The EV glided along the road once more, this time with Amorina curled against my side.

As symphonic music scored our trip, I mused on my personal journey with Amorina.

Two years ago, she had been the first person to extend her hand in friendship, seeing me as an evolving personality full of potential rather than fearing me as someone strange and unknown as others did. Since then, she'd become so much more to me: a friend, a confidant, a voice of reason, and a lover. As I looked out the window at the passing farmland, I smiled. She didn't know it yet, but I'd applied to be given a farm to manage – a place where we could be together and that we could call our own. The EV rounded the next corner, and the township came into view; built around the remnants of the founding colony ship, it was the central hub for all the surrounding farmlands.

❈❈❈

"Is there anything else you'll be needing, young master Raith?" asked one of the shop keepers.

"Um … possibly," I said, glancing at him. "Has my father produced enough to get one of these?" I asked, pointing to the stand of Arachnobot Fives, newly arrived from Earth.

"Let me check for you," the keeper said as he went over to a terminal.

I grabbed one of the Arachnobots off the shelf. They were robotic devices capable of operating as either a smartwatch or a spiderlike robot.

"Your father does have enough produce on record, but it will use your entire annual surplus."

"That's fine. Everything on the farm is in good working order. We can afford to spend a little."

I pocketed the Arachnobot, then turned and walked out of the building. I checked inside the EV, ensuring all the farm supplies were loaded in, and then glanced around for Amorina.

"Raith," I heard her voice calling over the noise of the town. "Raith! Over here!"

I spotted Amorina on the other side of the road at her mother's coffee shop. As I walked over, she pushed a seat out with her foot.

"Do you want a coffee?"

"Yeah, sure."

"I thought you might. Mum is already making your favourite."

I smiled as I sat down, appreciating Amorina's foresight.

"How's yours?"

"Perfect," she said, taking another sip, "as always. Mum's never made a bad one yet."

Amorina's mother made fantastic coffee, and my mouth began to salivate at the thought of my own taste of perfection arriving.

"Did you get something for yourself, as you mentioned?"

"Yeah, I did. Remember that old Arachnobot that I've got back at the farm?"

"Yeah. What about it?"

"In the store, they had fifth-generation ones fresh from Earth. So I got one."

Amorina chuckled. "You know they only send us their outdated tech, right? Plus, it takes like two years for it to get here from Earth, so they're always a generation or two ahead."

I nodded. "Yeah, but it's still an upgrade for me."

"Raith! Good to see you again."

I looked up as Amorina's mother placed a coffee in front of me.

"Hi, Anne! Good to see you too. How're things?"

Anne beamed at me with the same smile that I had so often seen grace Amorina's face.

"Things are good. A steady flow of customers and a happy, healthy daughter – what more could I want?"

"More customers?" I said with a wink.

Anne laughed. "Well, I certainly wouldn't say no!"

Suddenly, a rumble permeated the air, coming from somewhere high in the sky. A chilling silence fell over the town as all laughter and conversation ceased, and people turned their gazes upwards. As Amorina looked up as well, I watched the blood drain from her face.

"What is it? What's happening?" I asked, glancing upwards.

"It might be nothing … maybe just a meteor," said Anne unconvincingly, her face equally pale.

I looked around at the townsfolk, all staring at the sky, fear written across their faces.

"You're telling me people are this concerned over a meteor?"

Anne turned to look at me. "You'd better fucking hope it's just a meteor!" she snapped.

My eyes widened in shock "Why? What's the alternative?"

A boom erupted from the sky, and the surrounding crowd gasped as people started pointing. I looked up to see eight points of light descending.

"Dropships!" someone shouted – a cry soon echoed by others.

Moments later, the light disappeared, revealing the dark metallic shuttlecrafts.

"What do dropships mean?" I asked
"It means," Amorina said, turning towards me with a tear-stained face, "it's a Soul Harvest!"

Chapter 2
The Soul Harvest

2146, Common Era – Planet Gaia, Outer Rim, Tynan Empire

"Raith, listen to me!" Anne shouted, grabbing my shoulders and pulling me to my feet. "You need to take Amorina now! Take her and run as far as you can. Hide. Hide and don't come out until you see the ships leave. Do you understand?"

"Yes, I understand! But what's a Soul Harvest?"

"There's no time for questions! Go. Go now! Both of you!"

We leapt to our feet, running over to the EV as the dropships' paths diverged overhead.

"Raith, they're going to surround the city!" Amorina yelled as she climbed in.

"I know! Vehicle, drive to our place, now!"

"Commencing journey to our place."

The EV started moving down the road, respecting the town's speed limits. I knew we'd never make it out before the dropships landed.

"We need to go faster …!"

"I know," I muttered back.

"What?" Amorina asked.

"Nothing. Vehicle, drive faster!"

"I am already travelling at the maximum speed allowed by this zone."

"Vehicle, drive faster! That's an order!"

"I am already travelling at the maximum speed allowed by this zone," the EV insisted again.

"We need to go faster!"

"I know!" I yelled, fighting the inner darkness.

"Then do something about it!"

"I can't! The vehicle won't disobey the speed limits!"

"Weakling!" the darkness snarled at me inside my head as it took control.

"Empirical override forty-two – get us out of the city limits at maximum speed."

The words came out of my mouth, but it was not my mind controlling them. As the darkness relinquished its control, the EV accelerated.

"Watch out!" Amorina screamed.

Ahead of us, people dived out of the way as the EV sped through the streets. There was a sickening crunch as first one person, then another, failed to dive out of the way. Amorina screamed with each impact as another two people fell victim to the speeding vehicle. But I was frozen in shock, my own scream trapped in my throat as the car continued its destructive path. The command I'd given appeared to have overridden not only the EV's speed but also its safety systems. As another bloodcurdling impact burned itself into my memory, I wondered how I'd come to know such a command.

"Make it stop!" Amorina screamed.

"Vehicle, stop!"

The EV's brakes slammed on, locking the wheels, and skidding down the street. After several metres, it came to a stop, just on the outskirts of the town. To our horror, we watched as a dropship touched down in front of us.

"Shit, shit, shit, shit!" Amorina yelled as its doors opened and Imperial soldiers exited.

As the soldiers fanned out and a group started running towards us, I figured now was as good a time as any to understand what was happening.

"Amorina – I still don't understand. Why are they here? What does it mean?"

"It's a Soul Harvest!"

"Yes, that's been mentioned! Still doesn't mean I understand what that is!" exasperation was seeping into my voice along with the strain of what had just occurred.

"The Empire is going to kidnap people to be used as labourers, soldiers, skilled workers, and sex slaves. It happens every three years or so. I'm surprised your parents didn't talk to you about this – it's what happened to Livietta, after all."

"Wait – Livietta – the reason she's gone is that she was taken during a Soul Harvest?"

"Yes!"

As the gravity of Amorina's explanation sunk in, the soldiers started banging on the EV.

"Come out willingly, or we'll extract you by force!" a soldier shouted at us.

"We should get out," Amorina whispered.

I nodded, hoping that if we cooperated it would go smoother and Amorina would be unharmed.

"Vehicle, open the doors."

As the doors opened, multiple hands reached into the interior, grabbing hold of Amorina and I, throwing us onto the dirt outside.

"Take them into the centre!"

More hands grabbed us, hauling us to our feet and marching us back into the town. Carefully glancing left and right, I observed the soldiers more closely. Their dark form-fitting suits and full-face helmets hid the people within, a dehumanising tactic to increase their intimidation. Each soldier appeared to be carrying a rifle and a handgun.

On the left shoulder of the uniforms was the Empire's insignia. It was in the shape of a shield: red-tipped black wings creating the sides, and a fist rising through the middle grasping onto a banner, with the words "Per Unitatem Nos Ortum" written across it, forming the top of the shield.

"Through unity, we rise ..."

Great, I thought, the darkness can translate Latin. Wait, how did I know it was Latin?

As we walked into the town centre, I saw that most townsfolk had been detained, sitting in a group surrounded by soldiers.

"Line them up!" someone barked behind me.

The soldiers complied quickly, hauling people to their feet and shoving them into line, Amorina and I among them.

"Begin the assessments!"

The soldiers began moving along the line, checking each person for unspoken criteria. One soldier stood out in front of the crowd, presumably the commanding officer, watching as the assessments took place. The soldiers were neither kind nor careful with their evaluations, dropping the men's trousers and tearing off their shirts, then hastily checking their genitals and squeezing their arms and legs. Mouths were pried open, ears yanked, and eyes held open. The women fared no better – the soldiers tore off their skirts and dresses, groping breasts and probing between their legs.

I watched with dumbfound horror; I'd never witnessed such poor treatment of fellow human beings before.

"Lies ..."

Fine, I thought, I can't remember ever having witnessed this.

My disbelief continued as not a soul objected to the unfolding chaos. As one of the soldiers arrived before Amorina, I knew I couldn't stay silent.

"Leave her alone!" I yelled out.

As I went to take a step forward, a fist connected with my jaw, snapping my head back, but before I could recover, a second fist slammed into my gut. As I doubled over, a pair of hands grabbed my head, pulling it up and driving it down onto their knee. I felt my nose break with a sickening crunch and was shoved aside. I collapsed to the ground, pain surging through my body.

So that's why nobody objects, I mused.

As I tried to stand, I felt a boot plant itself in-between my shoulders, holding me down.

"What is she to you, shitface? Your wife? Your girlfriend?" asked the owner of the boot.

I wondered if they would treat her better or worse, knowing we had a connection.

"Fine, don't answer me. But you're going to watch."

True to his word, he yanked my head up by the roots of my hair and held it so I had a clear view of Amorina.

I watched as they subjected her to the same cruel treatment that the other women had experienced, albeit with the soldier's hands lingering longer and squeezing harder. As soon as they let her go, the boot came off my back, and the hand released my hair with a shove, banging my head on the packed earth.

"Get up – get back in line!"

I slowly rose to my feet and stumbled back into the line.

"Pathetic …"

Yep, I thought, just the positive affirmation I needed.

"All right, let's keep moving. Persons nine zero seven, one two eight, five five nine, four eight five, four seven, one two three, six one two, and two two one – labourers," the Commander ordered.

Several soldiers moved forward, grabbing eight people from the line. Presumably the numbered individuals that'd been called out – although I wondered when and how we were assigned numbers.

The soldiers led the selected eight down the road, back towards the dropships. The Commander called out two more groups of eight, designated as soldiers and skilled workers.

"Finally – two two seven, one eight nine, four two nine, six seven three, nine four six, four nine, five one four, two zero four, five zero five, and six eight five … sex slaves."

The soldiers moved forward, and my heart dropped as I watched them walk up to Amorina.

"No!" I cried out, rushing toward her. "Leave her alone!"

Before I'd made it two metres, I was grabbed by the neck and yanked backwards. Then they kicked me in the back, and I fell forward onto my knees. Someone grabbed a fistful of my hair, pulling my head back and pressing a knife to my throat.

"And why in the hell should we do that, shitface?"

I glanced to my right and saw the Commander coming closer.

"Why should we leave her alone?" he asked as he approached.

"Because she's a human being. They're all human beings. Not just objects you can come and claim when you feel like it."

A wave of laughter swept through the soldiers and the Commander as he stopped before me.

"See, that's where you're wrong. This world, Gaia, isn't a United Earth Republic colony – it's a Tynan Empire colony, which means there's one key difference. You are not a citizen of the Republic, but you are the *property* of the Empire."

"No! You are my property …"

"Ergo, we can do whatever the fuck we want with any of you. Whenever, wherever, and for whatever reason we so deem!"

"Assert yourself! Claim your property!"

Now is not the time, I thought, trying to suppress the darkness.

"Command them!"

"Okay, well … take me instead. Leave her here and take me!"

Another round of laughter moved through the soldiers.

"You are thick, aren't you?" the Commander mused. "There isn't much demand for the likes of you for this designation. The Empire's commanders don't much like fucking white trash asshole."

I was at a loss. What now? I couldn't overpower the soldiers; they wouldn't take me in Amorina's place – how could I save her?

"Command them! Command your property!"

The problem with the darkness was it never took over if I wanted it to – only when I fought it could it take control. So I fought it.

"Command them!" it hissed, angrier than before.

No, I told it.

"Command them!" it cried, growing louder in my head.

No!

"Then I will command them!" and the control I had over my own body slipped away.

My mouth opened, air passed over my vocal cords, vibrating to produce my voice and yet the voice that came out wasn't mine; it didn't sound like me, and it didn't use my words.

"Attention, soldier! Be silent and obey me!" my voice held an air of authority that I had never heard myself use before.

The knife disappeared from my throat as all the soldiers and the Commander snapped to attention, as if by magic.

As quickly as the darkness had assumed control, it relinquished it, leaving me somewhat unable to issue a follow-up command. Breaking free from their momentary lapse of control, I was seized again, and the Commander backhanded me across the face.

"How the fuck did you just do that, you piece of shit?" he shouted.

My mind reached for any possible, rational explanation, but the only one it landed on was magic, so I shook my head, just as unable to answer the Commander as I was to answer myself.

Another backhand strike struck me across the face. "How the fuck did you do that?" he yelled, his face twisted with anger and confusion.

"Magic?" I replied, hoping to avoid another slap.

The Commander struck me again. "Don't get smart with me – how the fuck did you do that?"

"You command what you own ..."

Eh, what the hell, I thought, it's not like I had a better answer to give.

"You, ah ... you command what you own?" I replied.

The Commander's eye twitched, and I watched his hand curl into a fist.

Well, this went about as well as I thought, I mused, as his fist came flying towards me.

♨

"Raith? Raith? You need to wake up. Raith! Wake up!"

As a voice started to register in my brain, I realised I was lying prone on the ground and that the commander's punch must've knocked me unconscious.

My brain was cycling through its start-up tasks like a computer, reorienting itself with the conscious world and its place in it.

"Raith! Wake up, god damn it!"

As if my speech recognition had come online, I realised Anne was speaking to me.

"Wusth 'appenin'?" I managed to slur out.

"Listen to me! If you want to save Amorina, you need to get up now!" Anne shouted.

Save Amorina – yes, I thought, I want to do that. "Help me up," I said, reaching out a hand.

Anne took my hand, pulled me to my feet, and then ushered me towards an awaiting vehicle.

"What are we doing?"

"Get in! I'll explain on the way," Anne responded, shoving me into the vehicle.

She climbed in behind me, ordered the vehicle to start and then pulled my face towards her. "Listen to me, and listen to me good, Raith. The soldiers, they will have loaded the prisoners onto the dropships by now and be preparing to lift off. When we get close, I'll create a distraction, and you'll sneak aboard the ship. Are you following me so far?"

"Yeth."

"Repeat what I just said to you."

"You'll be a dithtraction," I shook my head to clear the lingering fog, "and I'll sneak on the ship."

"Close enough," Anne said with a sigh. "Keep listening. Chances are you won't have time to find Amorina – hell, you might not even be on the same ship – but you should go to the same place. Find her and then find a way back. Do you understand?"

"Yes."

"Promise me, Raith – swear to me that you'll bring my daughter home! Otherwise, she'll end up just like your sister."

Whilst the knowledge of Livietta's abduction was still new to me, I knew that she'd never made it home, and I didn't want the same fate for Amorina. "I swear it – I'll bring her home."

"Thank you, Raith," Anne said as the vehicle came to a stop.

"Alright, we're here." She picked up a glass bottle with a rag coming out the top.

"Is that … is that a Molotov cocktail?"

"You know what a Molotov cocktail is?" Anne asked with an eyebrow raised.

"Yeah … apparently. Why? Is that unusual?"

"Molotovs are old knowledge, forbidden really. I'd say you'd be hard-pressed to find many people who know what they are. Anyway, we're wasting time. Wait until the soldiers have left the dropship to chase me and then get on."

Anne stepped out of the vehicle and started moving towards the ship. "Hey, arseholes! Come get me, you sons of bitches!" she yelled, lighting the Molotov's rag.

With an overarm throw, she hurled the cocktail towards the ship. As the glass shattered, the liquid inside spilled out across the ground, then the flames took hold, igniting with a "woof."

"Come on, you motherfuckers!" Anne screamed.

A dozen soldiers exited the dropship, sprinting towards Anne. They reached her and started beating her with the buttstocks of their rifles. As her muffled cries rang out, I wanted to help her, but I knew this was my chance. I stepped out of the vehicle and sprinted towards the dropship, checking to see if the soldiers had spotted me, but Anne was still the focus of their attention.

Arriving at the dropship, I ran up the ramp and stepped inside and found four rows of cryopods, eight of them filled with prisoners.

I peered through the glass of each pod, but none of them contained Amorina. I ran back to the ship's entrance and looked out, seeing that the soldiers had begun to walk back. I glanced around the ship again, this time spotting the gear storage along the outer walls.

Scanning through the shelving, I spotted what I needed – a soldier's uniform.

I yanked on the trousers and the jacket, then headed for the nearest cryopod.

How does this thing work? I wondered as I studied the controls.

"*Red initiation switch, wait for cycle selection, choose route default …*"

I flicked what I hoped was the initiation switch and let out a sigh as the screen lit up. I tapped on the screen and selected the default route. The door to the cryopod swung open, and I climbed inside.

"*Hit the green activation button …*"

I reached outside of the pod and hit the activation button. Sure enough, the door swung shut, and a mask lowered itself down onto my face. As the temperature inside the pod plummeted, an extremely sour liquid started pouring into my mouth. Unable to stop the flow of fluid, it streamed into my lungs. This must be what it's like to drown, I thought.

Whether it was the cold or something in the liquid, drowsiness rapidly enveloped me, and the darkness chuckled. "*Sleep well … weakling!*"

Chapter 3
The Place Between Worlds

2147, Common Era – Machina Station, Mid Rim, Tynan Empire

I couldn't remember having experienced cryosleep, and yet it felt so familiar; perhaps it was part of my forgotten past, or just the echoes of old astronauts recalling their experiences. On Gaia, I'd listened to their recollections many times that cryosleep felt like a long, dreamless sleep. But my slumber was not dreamless. I spent my time in the ocean of darkness, alone and drowning in the turbulent waters as I had done every night on Gaia. The difference was that I could escape my nightmares at home when each morning dawned. But in cryosleep, there were no mornings, and so my nightly hell had transformed into an endless loop: I would drown, then find myself on a beach coughing up seawater, only for the waves to pick me up and sweep me out once more to begin the cycle again.

Finding myself coughing up liquid once more, I thought it was another cycle of the dream until I heard a voice.

"That's it mate, cough all that shit up."

I looked up, surprised to see a grizzly older man sitting before me.

With another retch, and another lungful of liquid expelled, I asked, "Who are you?"

"Names Arty," he replied.

"I'm Raith," I said, clearing my throat and wiping the cryo juice off my face. I winced as I ran my hand over my nose, discovering that my nose still felt bent and swollen.

"Mate, that looks like you took a fair knock."

"How long was I asleep? Should I not've healed?"

"You were out for a year, but mate, you're basically an ice block in these contraptions – as far as your body knows, you're carrying on from your yesterday!"

I nodded. "Right, that makes sense." I looked around at the other now empty pods. "Where are we, Arty?" I asked, continuing to wipe off cryo juice.

"We're aboard Machina Station, but surely you knew you were coming 'ere, right?"

"Um …" I muttered, trying to recall what I knew about Machina Station. "Not really."

"Where'd you come from?"

"Gaia. The soldiers came and took a whole bunch of people … including someone dear to me."

Glancing down, I realised I was still wearing a soldier's uniform.

"I'm not a soldier!" I said, starting to unzip the jacket.

"I know, mate – don't you worry," Arty replied, reaching out and stopping my jacket removal.

"You … you know?"

"Well, for starters, you're missing most of the uniform, aren't you? The jacket was a smart move, enough to fool most people at a glance, but anyone givin' you a closer look would know you wasn't the full package."

"Are you going to report me?"

"Mate, if I were gonna report you, we wouldn't be sittin' here right now."

"Why aren't you reporting me?"

"Mate, you startin' to sound like you want me to report you." He raised an eyebrow at me.

"No!" I exclaimed. "I don't mean to sound ungrateful … I'm just trying to understand you."

"Fair 'nuff – well, I'm a member of the Insurgency, and that sure as shit means I ain't no friend of the Empire.

It strikes me that any fool dumb enough to sneak aboard an Imperial dropship probably isn't a friend of the Empire neither."

"Ah, well, you'd be right there."

"First time?"

I raised an eyebrow. "First time what?"

"You know – takin' an icy nap?"

Oh right, I thought. I momentarily entertained the idea of explaining my amnesia and the likelihood that I'd done this before but had no recollection of doing so but decided against it.

"Yeah, the first time. Can you help me? I need to find that someone I mentioned … they'll be on one of the dropships that arrived when mine did."

"Sorry mate … I've stuck my neck out as it is, getting you outta your pod 'n' waking you up. Best I can do is take you before the Insurgency leaders 'ere on the station."

Better than nothing, I supposed. "Yes, please," I replied.

With a pained grunt, Arty stood and then offered me his hand. I took hold, and he pulled me up.

"Follow me," he said.

※ ⸜(˙▾˙)⸝ ※

As I followed Arty through the corridors of Machina Station, I used the trip to observe my surroundings. Each hallway was industrially designed, dimly lit and cold, making for a rather sombre journey. Passing a porthole, I stopped and pressed my face against it, staring out into the void.

"We're in space."

"Yeah, mate," Arty said, stopping and turning to look back at me.

"We're in fucking space!"

"Yeah, mate, I know – space. Big, empty, an' only one fuckin' metal wall between you and nothin'ness."

Outside the window was darkness, filled with a splattering of stars. It gave off the faintest vibe that reminded me of my nightmares. But here, staring out into space, I felt no fear of drowning; instead there was a sense of peace that filtered through my body.

"Come on, mate, best we keep movin', aye?" Arty called out.

"Yeah … Hey, this place, it just … it floats out here?"

"Pretty much. As I understand it, way back when the Empire had colonised the Inner Rim, they'd discovered the habitable planets in the Outer Rim but found nothing liveable in the Mid Rim. So, they built Machina, a vital link in their growing chain of colonisation."

"With the cryotech, couldn't they've just slept through the journey from Inner to Outer Rim?"

"I ain't no cryotech expert or nothin', but unless it's gotten better, most folks can't go more than a year in an icy nap. This station is a midway point – a year from Earth, a year from Gaia."

I turned to look out the porthole once more, taking in its vast and dark splendour.

"Come on, mate – we had best be gettin' on."

I carried on walking, following Arty through more of the station. For a midway point, it was a lot busier than anticipated. There were soldiers, of course, and plenty of people wearing similar uniforms to Arty, whom I assumed were the staff – maintenance workers, janitors, cleaners, etc. There were prisoners, too, including a few faces I recognised from Gaia. We finally arrived at a doorway, where Arty knocked four times.

Moments later, the door slid open, Arty stepped inside, and I followed. As the door closed behind me, I looked around at the new environment I found myself in.

In contrast to the hallways outside, the room was large, open, and warm. Two dozen faces were watching me intently, instilling a sense of unease within me.

"Who've ya brought in whit ya, Arty?"

"A stowaway from on-board one of the newly arrived dropships. He's no friend of the Empire."

Despite Arty vouching for me, a large man stepped forward and began frisking me. After a few moments, the frisker pulled out my still unopened Arachnobot.

"We've got an unclean device!" they yelled out.

A different man ran up and grabbed the Arachnobot, then raced off again.

"I don't understand … why's it unclean?"

"Quiet – you don't get to speak yet," the frisker replied.

Satisfied with his search, the man turned away from me and called out, "He's good, boss."

I looked around for the "boss", spotting them as they replied.

"I'll decide who is or is na a friend of the Empire, ye hear?" said a hulk of a man, leaning forward into the light. "Come forward, laddie," he added, beckoning me closer.

Arty gave me a shove, and I stumbled across the floor until I stood before my beckoner.

"State yer name."

"I'm Raith."

"Raith, who?"

"Just Raith, sir – I've no other names."

"De ye hear that, lads? He called me sir."

If it were possible for the already quiet room to grow more silent, it did. The sound waves abandoned the air for what felt like an eternity, adding to my earlier unease. Then the big man broke out into thunderous laughter, and the crowd followed. Feeling calmer, I let out a chuckle.

"Did I say ye could laugh?" the big man inquired, returning the room to a state of silence.

"N-no," I said, almost adding sir again. "My apologies."

"Righto … Mr Raith, tell me, where've ye come from?"

"Ah, from Gaia. Farming district 42. I farmed, funnily enough."

"Did I ask ye what ye did?"

I shook my head.

"Right, well dinna answer questions ye weren't asked."

I nodded, noticing that my palms had become sweaty.

"Arty said ye were stowed away aboard an Empire dropship. How come?"

"The Empire came to Gaia to do a Soul Harvest ... they took my partner, Amorina. Her mother helped distract the soldiers, and I snuck aboard, slipped on part of a uniform, and jumped into a cryopod, to try and rescue Amorina."

My interrogator nodded, a thoughtful look on his face.

"You left to command!" hissed an unwelcome voice.

I realised this was the first time the darkness had spoken since awakening from cryosleep – why'd it been so silent for so long?

"Not now," I muttered under my breath.

"What was that?"

"Sorry ... I just said where now – I was wondering where Amorina was now."

"Aye, well, stop wonderin' and just answer my questions. What's wit' the scar on yer head?"

I reached up and ran my fingers across the scar that circled my head. "We believe I was operated on, but we don't know for certain."

"What was the op for? Whose we? An' why aren't ye certain?"

"I don't know because for whatever reason it was done, it left me with extreme brain trauma. I don't remember anything prior to two years ago. We being my doctor."

"De ye know anything, anything at all, about yer life from before?"

"Only that I'd come from off-world – relative to Gaia that is – as the doctor said that the technology used to operate wasn't present in the Outer Rim worlds."

"One last question: the bruisin' on yer face, and yer broken nose – how'd ye get those?"

"During the aforementioned Soul Harvest, some of the soldiers took objection to *my* objections."

The big man leaned back into the shadows, and the room remained silent. I didn't know whether this was good or bad, but I was growing more nervous by the minute.

"Assert yourself, weakling! Command them before they command you!"

I cocked my head slightly, willing the darkness inside to dissipate.

"Assert yourself!" it yelled louder.

I closed my eyes, focusing. The last thing I needed right now was for it to take control. A sudden outburst wouldn't help my case right now.

"Assert ..." it started to yell once more, but then the big man leaned forward. "I've decided that Mr Raith here ... is na a friend of the Empire!" he exclaimed.

The room gave a cheer and returned to their conversations, the spectacle of my interrogation seemingly over.

The big man reached out a hand. "The names Ally McDougal, laddie, but folks round 'ere call me Doug."

I shook Doug's hand. "It's ah – nice to meet you."

"Aye."

"Might I ask a question, now?"

"Aye, laddie, but make it quick. Ye interrupted my drinkin' with yer arrival, an' I'm keen to get back."

"Can you help me find Amorina? She must be on the station too, right? People can't go more than a year in cryosleep, so they'd have to wake her up before carrying on?"

"It's true, they'd have woken her, but twelve hours is all the time they need between wakin' up an' goin' back to sleep. It'll not be long before she's away again, laddie."

"We need to find her now then!"

Doug grimaced and shook his head. "I canna do that. The Insurgency has a purpose, an' that is to take doon the Empire. I'll not risk my men for the sake of one woman. I understand what she means to ye, but we must all make sacrifices."

"Then let me go and find her."

"I canna let ye out right now neither."

"Why not?"

"Because right now, it's the dead of night in those halls. There was enough risk in Arty bringin' ye here, and he knew the station. On yer own, yer as good as lost, and if ye run into a patrol, it'll be bad news for the lot of us."

"So what I am to do then?"

"Ye'll stay here fur the night. Arty will show ye to a room. In the morn', we'll send ye on ye way."

I could tell arguing would get me nowhere, so I nodded. "Thank you."

I felt a tap on my shoulder and turned around to see Arty standing there.

"Come on, mate. I'll take you to your room, yeah?" he said, also handing over my Arachnobot.

I nodded. "Hey, ah … what did they do to this?" I asked, holding up the device.

"The lads' jailbroke it – took off the Empire's spyware and unlocked its full functionings."

I nodded again, and Arty started to lead me away. As I followed, the darkness had one last thing to say.

"Fool! You've let yourself be commanded."

I sat in my lodgings for the night, musing over my frustration at the situation. Amorina was on-board the station, but two dozen men stood between me and my opportunity to find her – two dozen men that wouldn't let me leave until morning.

Amorina would have been refrozen and shipped further towards the core worlds by that time. I needed a plan. If I couldn't get to Amorina now, the best I could do was find out where she was being taken to and follow.

I needed to build an inventory of what I had, so I searched my pockets.

As I pulled out my father's shopping list and his EV keys, his words echoed in my head – "It's my job to refocus you. To remind you of which wolf to feed." – and I realised I missed him. What I wouldn't give for him to be here right now, to sit down beside me and set the world straight. In the two years that I'd known him, he had treated me like a son.

Reaching into my other pocket, I pulled out the Arachnobot. This time Amorina's voice was the one to echo through my mind. "You know they only send us their outdated tech, right? Plus, it takes like two years for it to get here from Earth, so they're always a generation or two ahead." I smiled, realising that thanks to having taken a ride in my pocket for the last year, it was another year out of date.

"Let's see what you can do," I said, opening its dishevelled packaging. I really hoped that the Insurgency's jailbreak hadn't damaged the device like they had its box.

As I held it in my hand, it vibrated momentarily, then its rectangular shape split and started to transform into its signature namesake form. Its singular body split into five pieces, then four of them split again, creating eight legs. It's eye like sensors at the front of its cephalothorax lit up blue, and the legs creased at the joints, pressing into my palm as it stood. The screen that ran along the back of its abdomen illuminated, flashing a greeting message.

Hello! I am an Arachnobot Five. Would you like to give me a name?

A name, aye? I wondered what would make a good name, then shuddered as the darkness awoke.

"The itsy bitsy spider crawled up the waterspout," it drawled slowly.

It felt like the voice was reciting something, but I didn't know what, nor did I want to keep listening.

"Bitsy! Your name is Bitsy!" I blurted.

"Spoilsport ..."

Blissfully unaware of the voice inside my head, the Arachnobot jittered happily in my hand.

Bitsy – I like it!

I smiled as I looked down at the little gadget. I got the feeling I was going to like the little fella.

What would you like me to do?

"What can you do?"

I come with several default functions, including observation and data access, companionship, and timekeeping.

"What sort of observation and data access can you do?"

I can record footage and audio and access information from nearby digital networks and devices.

"Can you demonstrate, please?"

Of course! One moment.

The screen went blank, and Bitsy jittered around, tilting its cephalothorax from left to right as if to indicate it was thinking. After a few moments, its screen lit up again.

I accessed the station's wireless network and ascertained its basic information and location. Machina Station is an imperial station, J-Class design, zero point three of a parsec from Lalande 21185, a red dwarf star in the Mid Rim of the human domain.

I nodded, impressed by what Bitsy had found. I wondered how capable it was and decided to try my luck.

"Can you access any records for a young woman named Livietta? She probably passed through the station seven … maybe eight years ago, originally from Gaia?"

Bitsy jittered in my hand briefly before its screen lit up once more.

Livietta Rosworth was onboard this station on the day 07-01-2139. She was taken to Terranova, where she remained until her death on the day 27-09-2141.

Terranova – so that's where she'd ended up.

"How did she die?"

She was strangled to death by the Empire commander she was providing sexual services to.

I made a mental note: if I ever made it back home, I needed to tell my parents the truth of what had happened to Livietta. I just hoped it would provide them with some measure of closure.

"Thank you, Bitsy. I need you to do something else for me. I'm looking for a woman who should be on this station and will be shipped off soon. Her name is Amorina. Do you think you can find out which ship she is due to go on and where it will take her?"

Bitsy jittered in my hand again before displaying another message.

I cannot access that information wirelessly – I will need to find a hard-line. Place me in the vent above, and I will find one. Then I will return.

I looked up to see the vent Bitsy spoke of. Standing on the bed, I lifted the Arachnobot up, and it crawled through the gap. I listened to its metallic footsteps as it walked off before lying back down. I hoped Bitsy would find her and learn what I needed so I could follow her in the morning.

Chapter 4
A Shift in the Wind

2147, Common Era – Machina Station, Mid Rim, Tynan Empire

I woke up to the metallic ring of Bitsy's footsteps above me, and I stood to pull it out of the vent.

Hello! read the message on Bitsy's screen.

I knew it was only a gadget, but as I watched it jitter about on my hand for a moment, I smiled. It felt like a pet – a living, intelligent creature with mannerisms and personality – and it struck me at how incredible that was for a machine to imitate life.

I was able to find Amorina. She was placed back into cryosleep two hours ago, aboard dropship DS-3956, which has been loaded onto a frigate bound for Terranova.

"How can I get to Terran–"

A knock at the door interrupted my questioning.

"Watch mode!" I whispered to Bitsy.

The Arachnobot obliged quickly, scurrying over to my wrist. Four of its legs swung forward, four swung back, wrapping themselves around my wrist. Its abdomen display dimmed, displaying the date and time in digital format, just as the door to the room slid open.

"Good mornin', laddie! Glad to see yer up! Come on, we've got to get you movin'!" Doug greeted, standing in the doorway.

"Get moving where?"

"After yer lassie!"

"Why? Yesterday you made it clear you wouldn't help me."

"Aye, well, a lot can change in a few hours. Ye ken?"

I followed Doug out into the hall, suspicious of the change of heart.

From my limited experience with Doug and the Insurgency, they didn't seem like the types to change their minds – least of all for reasons such as my own – it wasn't worth their time serving the needs of the one when they aimed to help the many.

"So, what's the plan?"

"We found yer lassie; she's bound for Terranova. We've arranged ye a cryopod in a dropship that'll be loaded onto the same frigate."

"What's on Terranova?"

"Terranova is a … pleasure world, if ye like. An Empire controlled planet where the Earth Republic's rich an' the Empire's faithful wine, dine, an' indulge. All the food ye can eat, an' all the flesh ye can fuck!"

My stomach sank as I processed Doug's last sentence. I remembered how the Empire had treated people during the Soul Harvest, and I couldn't believe they'd treat you any better once they'd forced you into being a labourer or a sex slave. Amorina didn't deserve that – hell, nobody did! I knew I needed to try and save her from that dark fate. I only hoped I could find her in time.

"Now pay attention, laddie – there's one thing we ask of ye."

Here we go, I thought, my suspicions confirmed. "Yes?"

"It's vital to the Insurgency that this key," Doug said, holding up a hardware encryption key, "gets to our agents on Terranova. They know yer comin', so once ye wake up on the other side, they'll find ye. Any questions?"

"Get this key to the Insurgency agents on Terranova – easy," I said, taking the key.

"Very good, laddie. An a wee bonus fur ye, they'll help ye find yer lass once they've got the key. Now go!

Arty will lead ye through the station an' get ye frozen again. Good luck!"

"Are you ready, mate?" Arty asked.

I jumped at Arty's sudden appearance.

"I guess so," I replied, glancing behind Arty to try and see where he'd come from. "Oh, wait! Can I get something to eat?"

"I've got just over an hour to get you to the dropship, so I'll find you a bite on the way, mate."

\\\(v)\\

The journey through the station corridors was the same as it had been the day before. The primary difference was that it was much busier. In addition to the soldiers and prisoners, there seemed to be many more civilians today.

"Why's it busier, Arty? Who're all these civilians?"

"They're travellers, mate. Either the rich, paying their way to explore the Empire's worlds, or skilled workers sent by the Empire from one place to another, carrying out specialised jobs."

That seemed plausible enough, but I wondered how much "specialised work" there was to do on the Empire's worlds – after all, Gaia hardly seemed like a good candidate for space tourists.

"Where are they going? Gaia isn't welcoming towards strangers."

"True that, mate, true that. Yeah, nah, they'll be either heading for Ares or destined for the exploration missions – looking for habitable worlds beyond the Outer Rim."

Ares was the neighbouring world to Gaia, and by a neighbour, I meant that it took eight months to travel between them.

"Ares is a military world for the Empire, right?"

"Yeah, mate. Trainin' soldiers, researching tech, and a launching ground for those exploration missions. All that food you produced on Gaia, Ares was your primary consumer."

"Who else did our food go to?"

"This station, of course!"

As we continued walking through the hallway maze, a voice suddenly stood out amongst the others.

"When is the frigate due to depart?"

"In about twenty minutes, sir."

They were the voices of a soldier and the commander – the same one from Gaia who'd assaulted me.

"Arty, hide!" I hissed, grabbing Arty from behind and pulling us both to the side.

As we crouched behind a crate, Arty looked at me. "What is it, mate?" he asked.

"The commander whom I encountered on Gaia, he's close!"

Arty nodded and scanned the crowd. After a few moments, the Commander and the soldier came into view.

"Any further updates on that shipment irregularity?" the Commander asked.

"Yes, sir – there was an additional person onboard dropship DS-2947. We reviewed the security footage to see when the individual was processed, but there was a system outage. We believe the Insurgency is involved," the soldier replied, the two of them walking closer to where Arty and I hid.

"That was the dropship you were on, mate," Arty whispered.

"Fucking insurgents! How've we not found their bloody rat's nest yet?"

"I don't know, sir."

"Of course you don't fucking know, you idiot. The question was rhetorical."

"Yes, sir – of course, sir."

I held my breath as the two men walked by, only taking in air once they'd passed the next corner.

"Come on, mate. Best we keep movin' – suspicious enough as is, the two of us crouched down 'ere."

Stepping out from our cover, we re-joined the crowd, moving towards my ride. Passing by a bakers' stall, Arty stopped.

"Still hungry?" he asked.

"Yes!" I exclaimed as my stomach voiced its opinion, letting loose a grumble that reached Arty's ears, causing him to chuckle.

"Oi, gov'na! Gives us a filled bun would ya?" he said, tossing a coin to the baker.

As the coin hit the baker on the head, she looked up, seemingly angry at first, but her face softened when she saw Arty.

"Oh, Arty, you ol' bugga! Charmin' as eva! 'Ere ya go!" She replied, tossing back a sandwich.

"Thanks, love!" Arty said, handing the sandwich back to me.

My stomach rumbled as I looked at the fresh warm bread with ham and lettuce poking out of the sides.

"Eat it!"

Duh, I thought, taking a bite. The flavours seemed to melt in my mouth, the ham and lettuce accompanied by previously unseen cheese and mayonnaise.

"Mmmmm!" I grunted happily.

Arty chuckled again. "Come on, mate – we've got a ride to catch!"

I nodded, following Arty as I took another bite of my meal.

❦

"You're late!"

The soldier standing before us was very large, and I was half-inclined not to argue any further.

"I know, mate, but what can you fuckin' do, aye?" Arty argued.

"I can stop you from boarding … because you're late," the soldier replied.

I felt like saying to Arty that he's got a point, but it seemed he had a response prepared.

"That may be true, but you'd be disobeying the commander's orders then, wouldn't you?"

The soldier narrowed his eyes. "Papers."

Arty pulled a chip out of his pocket and held it up for the soldier, who promptly scanned it.

"I see. Hurry up, get him on board and to sleep – I'll give you two minutes!" he snapped.

"Thank you," I said as Arty and I moved past.

I followed Arty into the dropship; the design was nearly identical to the previous one.

"What was the chip?"

"Your forged travel documents," Arty said, walking over to an empty cryopod.

"You guys can do that?"

"Mate – the Insurgency can do all sorts of things. We're pretty embedded within the Empire."

I nodded, watching Arty as he flicked the red initiation switch, waited for cycle selection, and chose route default. The door to the cryopod swung open.

"Climb on in," Arty said, offering me a hand.

I took it, allowing him to guide me into the pod, which, perhaps unsurprisingly, felt more comfortable than my rushed efforts last time.

"Now remember, mate, our agents will meet you on Terranova. They'll wake you, and you need to give them the key – you've still got it, aye?"

I patted my left-hand jacket pocket and nodded.

"Good work, mate. Any questions?"

"They'll help me find Amorina, right? Once I've given them the key?"

"That's right, mate."

"Okay … thank you, Arty, for all your help."

Arty nodded and gave me a sad smile. "Yeah, mate – no worries, aye? I hope you find your girl."

He hit the green activation button, and the door swung shut.

As the mask lowered itself down onto my face, I watched Arty walk away, leaving me alone with the dropping temperature.

"Not alone …"

Not again, I thought, remembering the torment of the last cryosleep. Can't you leave me alone?

"You command what you own … and I own you …"

A shiver ran through my body, but I couldn't tell if it was from the cold or the darkness's words.

"I assert myself … I assert control!"

A panicked feeling began to arise in my chest, and I could sense what was coming next. The sour cryo liquid started gushing into my mouth, down into my stomach and my lungs.

The darkness laughed. *"Drown!"* it hissed with glee.

As I choked on the solution, its effects began to kick in, and I felt the drowsiness wash over me. The darkness chuckled, and the world faded away.

❨❲ⅴ❳❩

"Hello, Raith …"

I woke up to find myself sitting on the familiar, stony beach of so many nightmares.

"I wanted to talk before I continue breaking you."

41

I looked to my left to see a human figure made of black smoke.

"Who are you?"

The smoky figure surged forward, stopping just before my face. *"Who do you think?"* it hissed.

The darkness – my darkness – in the flesh, or not, I supposed.

"What do you want?"

"You took everything from me. When you imprisoned me here on the shores I grew up on, I cried and screamed for hours, trying to escape, trying to break free! After an eternity on this beach, you tainted its memory, stealing from the little that remains!"

"Imprisoned you? I don't understand."

"You will … As time passed, I started to forget myself and this beach. The stars began to disappear from the sky, and the moon began to shrink until only the smallest waning crescent remained."

I looked up to see a familiar black sky and sliver of moonlight.

"I became so depressed, I would swim out into the ocean, intending to drown, but I couldn't bring myself to do it. So I'd grow angry, and my rage would whip up a thunderous storm!"

With a growing sense of horror, I began to realise where this story was going.

"And then, only then, at the height of the storm, after I'd fought wave after relentless wave, would my wish be granted and I'd drown … then do you know what happened?"

"You'd wake up on this beach, coughing up seawater."

"Exactly! And I'd swing back out to try it all again, hoping this time it'd work!"

I didn't know what the darkness was or how it came to be imprisoned in my head, but at last I understood the reason for my reoccurring nightmares – it was the darkness making me live through the same torment it had.

"That's when I knew I'd lost it … doing the same fucking thing over and over and over, expecting it to change somehow … for the repetition of mistakes with the expectation of change is insanity!"

"Look, I'm sorry that happened to you, but I'm sure we can find a way to resolve this – to end it."

"It ends when I break you; when I've driven you mad enough to trap you in here … forever!"

Chapter 5
Home of War and Sex

2148, Common Era – Planet Astarte, Inner Rim, Tynan Empire

Vomiting cryo liquid onto a hard metallic floor was the first sign that I'd broken free from hell. I glanced around, taking in the loading dock and the refuelling dropship I'd travelled in. A man and a woman were kneeling beside me.

"Get it out of your system, buddy!" the man said.

I coughed up more liquid, then sat back, finally able to breathe in some fresh air. Except the air wasn't fresh. It was dusty, dry, and carried a metallic taste with it. Doug had said Terranova was a pleasure world where the Empire's faithful wined, dined and indulged – surely the air would taste better than this.

"Are you able to walk? The longer we're in the open, the more likely we are to draw suspicion."

I nodded, and the man helped me up.

"Come on, let's go!" he said, leading me away.

The two Insurgency members took me through a maze of corridors. The duration of our walk led me to believe that the facility was vast, and when coupled with its industrial design, it seemed less and less likely that I was on a "pleasure world."

Rounding the next corner, a large set of doors opened at our approach. It was much brighter outside than in, and my eyes adjusted after a few moments.

Large fields full of soldiers training stretched out before me. Between the training grounds stood rows of buildings, some looking like factories producing vehicles and weapons, whilst others appeared to be barracks and offices.

I'd heard many a story of Ares, the neighbouring world to Gaia, and the current view looked just as the tales had described – not that I could be sure, having never been to Ares.

"What world is this?" I asked.

"There's no time for questions –" the man glanced around, "– we need to get to a safe house."

"What world is this?" I asked again, feeling the darkness stir within me as my anger grew.

"Seriously, no time. We can answer your questions once we get somewhere secure."

"Enough!" snarled the voice within. I wanted answers, and I knew who could get them.

"You will answer me!" the darkness commanded. "What world are we on?"

The man's face looked confused as an unfamiliar authority emanated from my voice, and after a moment's hesitation, he said, "Astarte ... we're on the planet Astarte!"

"Ah – Astarte! Good to be back ..."

I was still on the wrong planet, but at least I'd moved in the right direction – closer to Amorina instead of further away. As the man pulled me away, I clenched my fists – the Insurgency has some explaining to do.

ᚾᚹᚾ

As the door to the safe house closed behind us, I turned towards the Insurgency members. A third individual had joined them.

"The Insurgency promised me a ride to Terranova in exchange for delivering the key – why the hell am I on Astarte?" I asked perplexedly.

"Honestly, I don't know, buddy. We were told you'd be coming here with a key and then to send you onwards to Terranova. If you got told something different, sorry, but that wasn't my doing."

"So, wait, you were told to send me to Terranova?"

"Yes! As soon as you hand over the key, we'll take you back to the transport hub and get you on a 'Nova bound ride."

"He lies ..."

I didn't trust them, but I couldn't see myself getting off-world easily without their help. I pulled the key out from my left-hand jacket pocket and held it up. The lady took it from me, walking across the room and plugging the key into a terminal on a gun. A small LED strip on the gun turned from red to green.

"The key to the kingdom works! We've got access to every weapon on the planet!" she said.

"Great. You've got it — now, get me to a Terranova transport, please!"

The two male members stepped forward, grabbing me by my arms and dragging me towards the door.

"Wait! What are you doing?" I scrambled about trying to dig in my feet and halt their forward motion.

"Following our instructions."

With a coordinated shove, the men pushed me out onto the street.

"What about Terranova!"

"Yeah, we lied about that — not our problem, buddy."

And with that, the door to the safe house closed.

"Told you ..."

What now, I wondered, knowing I wasn't going to be able to break the door down. Before I could decide on a course of action, the sound of marching feet echoed through the street.

A patrol was coming. I glanced around and spotted an external stairway with some crates underneath. I ran over and sat behind the boxes, waiting.

A minute later, two dozen soldiers marched past, kicking up the dust as they walked by. It hit the back of my throat, creating an irritation. With the soldiers still in earshot, I fought to stifle a cough. Another minute passed, and I finally let the tickle free, hacking up the discoloured gunk.

I needed a plan. "Hey, Bitsy – you with me?"

My watch unwrapped itself from my wrist, transforming into my little companion.

Hello! I am with you.

"That's good. I – I need your help. I'm on the planet Astarte, but that's about all I know."

Bitsy jittered in my hand for a few moments.

Astarte, a military world for the Empire, named after the ancient near eastern goddess of war and sexual love. Located at the edge of the Inner Rim, its closest neighbour is Terranova.

"Are there transports that go between Astarte and Terranova?"

Yes – every day. The journey takes about two days.

I opened my mouth to ask about the subsequent transport, but Bitsy's display continued.

The next transport leaves this afternoon, in a few hours.

Smart little guy, I thought, pre-empting my questions.

"Can you reserve me a space, please?"

Of course. I'll modify your travel documents as well.

"What travel documents?"

The ones that Arty forged for you. I made a copy.

"Thank you, Bitsy! One last thing ..."

I'll revert to watch mode and display travel directions to the transport hub as you go.

The jailbreaking treatment that the Insurgency had provided was proving quite helpful.

"Thank you," I said, smiling as Bitsy wrapped itself around my wrist once more.

As the first set of directions scrolled across its display, I stood and began to follow them. Fuck the Insurgency, I thought, they wouldn't help me, but I didn't need them to – I'd make my own damn way to Terranova, save my girl, and return home. Simple, right?

༄༅།།༄

The walk back to the transport hub was quieter and less urgent than the earlier journey. I took in the world as I walked, trying to understand the sights and sounds it produced. The background noise was constant but varied as you moved through the different areas: a mix of mechanical sounds from the factories rumbling and hissing, and organic sounds from the soldiers shouting and grunting during their drills. Similarly, the air would reek of burnt metal and oil as I passed by the forges but stink of blood and sweat as I walked near the training fields. To me, a world utilised like this was sad and wasteful. I'd grown up on a farming world, filled with greenery and life, growing food that sustained lives. But here, these men and machines had one purpose: to take life, to destroy it.

"Your viewpoint is so narrow. Limited by the brief flash of life you've experienced. To me, this world is beautiful."

If you say so, I thought, but tell me, how is this beautiful?

"This rumbling, industrious world is the end product of a system that obeys without question, working without reward, a ceaseless war machine that shall provide the key to victory."

Before I could argue the point any further with the darkness, a door up ahead flew open, and an officer came flying out, losing his footing on the top step and crashing to the ground.

"Get out, stay out, and don't come back until you have some useful fucking information!" a familiar voice screamed from within the building.

The officer cringed as the door slammed shut, and he proceeded to wipe blood off his face. I stepped behind a corner, moving out of sight, and watched as the officer picked himself up and stumbled down the street. Once he'd gone, I moved closer to the building. I could hear voices from within and noticed one of its windows was ajar.

"The quality of these junior officers has gone to shit recently."

That was the Commander. The frigate he'd mentioned departing on had been the same one my dropship had travelled with – both bound for the same destination.

"His information was valid," a second voice said, perhaps belonging to another officer.

"Valid, yes, but also incomplete. I cannot act upon half-assed info!"

"It's the tenth report of forged travel documents we've had this month alone – the Insurgency is growing increasingly active, right under our noses. But still, we struggle to find and extinguish them."

"Granted, they're an annoyance, but that is all they are – I doubt they've any real power."

"What if they've got an ace they're just waiting to play at the opportune moment?"

"Then we'll counter it. The Empire has held power for over one hundred years for a reason."

"Yes, but the Insurgency's previous efforts affected us far less than a move might do now – they cannot be allowed to disrupt the invasion."

"Don't worry. The United Earth Republic will fall; Mars and Earth will belong to the Empire at long last, all of humanity united under a single banner. We cannot fail. They have a splattering of forces provided by their member states; we have two planets dedicated to creating an army."

"But what if ..."

"No!" the Commander yelled, slamming something. "There is no what if! There is only victory!"

The room fell silent, but the darkness piped up.

"The invasion lives!"

My heart clenched at the thought that the darkness knew of the invasion, another unexplained stain from my past. It was a bold move to invade Earth and Mars, and given the industrial scale of this world and the fact that it was one of two military worlds, it seemed plausible that the Empire could do it. And if the Republic were gone, the Empire's power would be absolute. I'd seen what it was like to live under that control, and I cringed at the thought of the Republic's freedoms disappearing.

"I'm not questioning you, sir, but what assurances do we have against the Insurgency?"

"The element of surprise. The Ares fleet will be arriving here tomorrow. When it does, travel will be suspended between the Empire's worlds. The Insurgency will not be able to send out physical messages. As they grow desperate, they'll use their digital channels, and then we'll know what their next moves are. With their counter plans crippled, we'll strike earlier than intended."

"How much earlier?"

"Seven months from now."

"That's ... that's an entire year ahead of schedule. Why've things been moved up?"

"The Emperor has commanded that it be so."

"Did he deliver the command himself, or did it come via the voice puppets again?"

"The advisors delivered the command, as usual."

"I'm telling you – the emperor is dead, and the advisors are running the show until his son comes of age!"

Concerningly, the darkness slowly chuckled, which it had never done before.

"I've told you before, Marshall, I will not indulge your conspiracy theories. Until proven otherwise, the emperor is alive and simply avoiding the public eye."

My mind swirled at all of this new information. The emperor, the emperor's son, the advisors, hastened plans and amassing forces – it was a lot to process. If all transport were blocked from tomorrow onward, the Insurgency would only have a small window to get this news to their leaders. Despite their betrayal, I knew I couldn't stand by as the Republic fell to the Empire.

I crept away from the window, rounding the corner quickly, where I ran into someone.

"Watch it!"

"My apologies!" I replied, realising it was the officer who'd gotten thrown out earlier.

"Why are you in such a hurry? Where'd you come from?" the young officer asked.

"Ah … nowhere, really, I was just, um … walking, out for a walk, yes. Yes, I was walking. Quickly."

"What's your rank and station, soldier?"

"Ah … Corporal of Munitions station – obviously."

As I spoke, I cringed internally. For all the authority that the darkness commanded, I projected none by comparison.

I heard the door open behind me. If the Commander saw my face, he'd undoubtedly recognise me. I sucker punched the young officer, delivering an uppercut into his solar plexus. As he collapsed, I turned and ran down the street – if I could lose the officers, I could warn the Insurgency.

I raced off down the street, but before long, I could hear his footsteps and laboured breathing behind me. I pushed harder, and the sounds grew fainter. I'd made it!

Suddenly an arm stretched out in front of me, clotheslining me. My head stopped, but my legs kept moving forward – lifting off the ground in front of me.

As the momentum kept my legs swinging up, I found myself looking at the sky. My arms started cartwheeling as I fell back towards the earth. The air was pushed from my lungs as I landed with a thud, accompanied by the sound of the joints in my back cracking. As the dust kicked up by my collision with the ground settled and I worked to catch my breath, I looked up at the figure standing over me.

"Well, well, well … who have we got here."

Chapter 6
"Where Do You Think You're Going?"

2148, Common Era – Planet Astarte, Inner Rim, Tynan Empire

The officers dragged me back to their office and bound me to a chair in the centre of the room. No one said a thing, but I could see that the junior officer was itching to say something. As the minutes passed us by, he finally gave in.

"This is the man from the forged documents that I told you about earlier, sir!"

"I know," sneered the Commander.

The room fell silent again. I decided to try my luck at a bluff.

"So guys, listen, I'm sure this has all just been some misunderstanding – I've got places to be; surely we can work something out?"

The Commander turned to look at me. "Where do you think you're going?"

"Terranova."

"Why would you be going there?"

"Ah, you know ... to have a pleasurable experience."

"If you were heading for Terranova, you'd have gone straight there from Machina Station, so why are you here?"

"A ticket mix-up, of all things! The travel agent fucked up. Typical, right?" I said with a shrug.

"You aren't used to lying, are you?"

"Lying? Who's lying? I'm not lying!"

The Commander rushed forward, grabbing the chair and tilting it backwards so that it hung on the precipice of falling over. "Stop lying to me! I am not a fool and will not be treated as such!"

With a little nudge, he let go, allowing me to topple over.

I tilted my head forward, sparing it from impact with the floor.

"Right," the Commander said calmly, "let's try this again. Where do you think you're going?"

"I am genuinely going to Terranova."

"Is the Insurgency sending you there?"

"The what now?"

I suddenly found myself righted and face to face with the Commander.

"The Insurgency. Did they send you?"

Not to Terranova, I thought.

"No. They didn't."

The Commander narrowed his eyes. "Where'd you get the forged documents from?"

"They were given to me by a stranger, on Gaia."

"Why?"

"So that I could get Amorina back."

"Who?"

"One of the women you seized from Gaia."

"Oh right – the one you got beaten for," the Commander said, grabbing my broken nose.

"Aaarrrggghhh!"

"She must be quite something for you to go chasing her across the galaxy. Most men would've simply found another wench to warm the bed."

"You're fucking disgusting, you know that?"

The Commander's fist smashed into the side of my face. I turned back towards him, spitting a tooth and bloodied saliva onto the floor. Inside, the darkness stirred.

"Enough of this ..."

Not now! I thought, trying to hold it back.

"Had enough ..."

Me too! But you can't help, so shut up!

"No ... had enough!"

I felt the darkness surge through my mind, seizing control.

"Commander Nathaniel Benjamin Moore of the Tynan Armies second division."

The blood drained from the Commander's face.

"How do you know my name?"

A taunting chuckle that carried an undertone of malice left my mouth.

"Oh, I know so much more about you than just a name."

"You're bluffing."

"How's your wife ... Samantha, doing? Or your daughter ... sweet little Julia?"

A look of recognition flashed across the Commander's face. "It can't be ..."

"Oh ... but you know it is," the darkness said, letting out another slow, menacing chuckle.

"I need to make a call. Keep a close eye on him," the Commander said, striding from the room.

As soon as he was out of sight, the darkness relinquished control, slipping back into the dark recesses of my mind.

The remaining two officers watched me closely. I wondered what they were thinking. What they thought of their commander, crumbling before the words of a stranger, a nobody. Did they fear me, as he did? Were they worried that I somehow knew who they were too? That I could name their wives and their children?

The Commander's voice rumbled through the wall, enough to disrupt the silence but too low to hear any words.

"Who the fuck are you?" asked the junior officer.

I glanced at the senior officer, who simply looked away – he knew better.

"I'm nobody, kid, nobody at all."

"Don't call me kid. A nobody doesn't come to know things like the name of Commander Moore. So you're either a spy for the Insurgency or a defector, maybe someone the Commander thought dead and gone. Which is it?"

"I'm Raith, a farmer from Gaia. That's it – there's no juicy story here, kid – sorry to disappoint!"

The officer moved towards me, fists balled, but stopped as the senior officer spoke up.

"Sit down and shut up, you idiot."

The junior officer reluctantly complied, returning to his seat.

I felt sorry for the kid. He wasn't wrong. Knowing the full names of the Commander, his wife, and his child was oddly specific information. Sure, I was Raith the farmer now, but I could've been a defector or a spy in the past – I couldn't remember either way.

The door opened, and the Commander walked back into the room, holding a large syringe.

"I asked you where you were going because you knew, and I did not." He grabbed my arm. "Now those roles have reversed. So, ask me. Ask me where you're going," he sneered, rolling up my sleeve.

"Where am I going?"

"To Earth," he said as he pressed the needle into my arm and emptied the syringe's contents.

"Earth? Why Earth?" I asked as my eyes grew heavy.

"Because the advisors will know what to do with you!"

Chapter 7
"You Know Me?"

2149, Common Era – Planet Earth, Inner Rim, United Earth Republic

I opened my eyes. The world around me didn't register with my brain, but the way I felt did: relaxed like I'd slept soundly for the first time in years. So, this must be what peace feels like, I mused. As my body woke up, details of my surroundings began to check in with my thoughts.

I was lying on a bed. It was large enough to fit at least five, maybe six people, and it was soft. I remembered my bed back on Gaia, how small and hard it'd been. This bed was on a different level though, with dark wooden posts at each corner, holding up a canopy of blood-red drapes. Bed curtains, I thought, weird.

"Not weird – this is what luxury looks like, you peasant!"

I breathed in deeply, suddenly aware of the scents in the air – like sweet citrus with an undertone of lavender, and yet, not quite. It was a beautiful smell, unlike anything I'd smelt before, a far cry from the earthen odours with which I was so familiar. As my brain continued to awaken, my memory came back online, and suddenly my thoughts were consumed by armies and insurgencies, soldiers and officers, worlds of war and planets of pleasure. I shot upright in bed, half expecting the three officers to be standing there, delighting in my panic as their mindfuck came to fruition. Instead, I was greeted by an enormous room.

"Holy fuck!"

I threw the blankets off and leapt out of bed, spinning around as I took in the splendour of the space. The red walls matched the bed drapes, divided up by gold accentuated marble columns. A hot tub was sunk into the polished marble floor, steam gently rising from its tempered waters.

I glanced up in awe at the golden chandeliers, seemingly miles above my head.

As I spun around, my eyes fell upon a colossal painting.

My mouth fell open. "What ... the ... fuck?"

It was me. Younger and without my scar, but unmistakably me. Red and gold robes hung from my body as I reclined on a lectus, a platter of fruit at my fingertips and a large apple in my hand. In the background sat a magnificent lake framed by snow-capped mountains. As I continued taking in the details of the painting, the door to the room silently swung open, and a young woman entered. She looked at me and averted her eyes downwards.

"Your Grace, forgive me – I was sent to fetch you."

"Nothing to be forgiven for," I said, no idea who she was or for whom she was fetching me, but I was ready to leave this room and hopefully get some answers. "Lead on!"

"Um ... Your Grace would perhaps like some clothing?"

I looked down and realised I was stark naked.

"Fuck! Please, forgive me ... I – I didn't realise I was naked!"

"That's okay."

We continued standing there in increasingly awkward silence as I hoped like hell that she'd tell me where I could find some clothing. When she remained silent, I spoke up.

"So, here's the thing – I don't know where any clothing is?"

"Oh! Over here, Your Grace," she said, moving past me.

Pressing on a wall panel, it popped outward, and with the slightest tug, the board glided silently to the side. It uncovered a large wardrobe within the wall, filled with clothing.

Standing there, dumbfounded by the variety on offer, it dawned on me that a single item of clothing from here was probably worth more than what my parents would make annually.

"What clothing would you like?"

"I ... I don't know, sorry."

"Perhaps you'd like your favourite?" she asked, pulling out a sweeping red and golden robe.

"Ah ... something simpler perhaps?" I replied, thinking myself quite pompous if I were to wear the robe on offer.

The young woman placed the robe back, rummaged around for a few moments, and pulled out a dark grey set of track pants and a hoodie lined with red velvet and gold thread. Still indulgent, but I was growing tired of covering myself.

"That'll do, thank you."

"I'll let you get changed, Your Grace. I will wait outside."

❦

True to her word, the young woman stood patiently outside the room as I exited it, donned in my new attire.

"This way, Your Grace," she said, leading me on.

"What's your name, if I may ask?"

She stopped, still ahead of me but partially turning her head to glance behind.

"I am Alyssa, Your Grace," she said quietly.

"Nice to meet you, Alyssa."

She nodded and kept walking, seemingly fearful of conversing with me. I'd noted her continued usage of "Your Grace" when addressing me. Paired with the painting on the wall and the fact that I had a "favourite robe", I had a past here.

"No ... I had a past here. You have nothing!"

Ignoring the darkness, I took to looking around the hallways as we walked, noting that the walls out here were marble, like the floors – quite a contrast to the richness of the red that adorned last night's chambers.

Every hundred metres or so, the left side of the hallway would open up into a courtyard.

Whilst each one was slightly different from the rest, they all shared some combination of gardens, seating, and pools. Those pockets of greenery breathed life into the otherwise artificial passageways.

"Who are you taking me to see, Alyssa?"

"The advisors."

"Who are they?"

"It is not my place to say. You will speak with them soon enough."

"You can tell me. I won't let anyone know you spoke with me if that helps?"

Alyssa quickened her step, seemingly to avoid me and any conversation. I reached forward, grabbing her wrist. She stopped and instantly brought her other arm up, covering her face as if ... as if to protect it. Like this had happened before – someone grabbing her and striking her. Had that been me? Had I done these things?

I let go of her arm. "Alyssa, I won't hurt you. Please, I just need some answers."

"I cannot give you what you seek!" she whimpered, turning and running away down the hall.

Great, I thought, now what?

A door slowly opened to my right, oversized and heavy, and it ground against the floor as it moved. As it opened, a group of seven old men came into view, all wearing dark grey robes with elaborate red patterns. One of the men stepped forward, a slight smile upon his face.

"Raith, isn't it?" he asked.

"Um ... yeah ... yes."

"Come inside. All the answers you seek will be revealed in due course."

The men parted to allow me through, and I moved forward into a cold and dark room, where black marble replaced the white marble found elsewhere. A lack of lighting further accentuated the darkness. These elements of the room enhanced its focal point: a solid circular plinth table, atop of which was embedded a holographic projector running from edge to edge. Its projection hovered in the air, displaying a wealth of information: video feeds, documents, and graphs.

"What is this place?"

"This is the hub of all our sensors. Our eyes and ears from all over the Empire, providing us advisors, the brain of the Empire if you like, with the data we need to make decisions."

I turned to look at the speaker, the same man who'd invited me into the room.

"And who are you?"

"I am Zavis. And these gentlemen are Phobus, Anwir, Biff, Avid, Chunta, and Lorcan."

Each man nodded in turn as Zavis introduced them.

"And you're all the advisors? On what do you advise? Who do you advise?"

"We provide advice on how to run the Empire. And we advise the emperor."

"Do you know me?"

"Intimately," Zavis said with a smile.

"Who am I?"

Zavis's smile faded. "You ... you have no idea?"

"What I know is that I'm a farmer from Gaia. My name is Raith. I don't know why I'm here or what you want with me."

"You are the missing Emperor Tynan Khidar, third ruler of the Empire."

"You're lying."

"I'm not. Your grandfather, Nicolas Frith, declared independence from the United Earth Republic after colonising Terranova. His son, your father, Khidar Nicolas, claimed additional territory, expanding into the Khidar Empire. And presently, it is the Tynan Empire, named after you."

"All of that means nothing to me! For all I know, that's just a fabrication!"

"That's fair. How about a detail I'm sure you've kept under wraps – the voice inside your head."

How did he know about that? Only my parents, the doctor, and Amorina knew about that.

"He knows it because he speaks the truth!"

"How ... how could you know that?"

"Because I know what it is. I know how you got it and where it came from, and I know what you can do with it. Perhaps it seemed like magic ... the way you could issue a command and be obeyed."

I opened my mouth to respond, before realising I didn't know what to say.

Zavis smiled. "As I said, I know you ... intimately."

"What is the voice?"

"That is better explained elsewhere. I can take you to the place where you both were created."

"Okay, assuming what you say is true and I am Tynan Khidar – what do you want with me?"

"That is ultimately your choice. You have absolute power here. What you decide is fact."

"There must be some options though, a preferable pathway you'd like me to follow?"

"Yes – ideally, you'd resume your mantle and become the emperor once more. Your subjects need to see you, for they've been losing faith. We need you to take command of what you own."

"And if I don't?"

"We'll let you go anywhere you want to."

No, they won't, I thought.

"No, they won't!" the darkness agreed.

"In my absence … you have all been running the Empire?"

"Yes, of course. That is part of our duty to you, to lead if you are otherwise occupied."

I remembered the officer's conversation back on Astarte, about the emperor's son.

"If I were absent, my son would surely rule in my place?"

"Ichirō is currently twelve years old. He was six when you vanished. In either case, he wasn't ready to rule. This is exactly why we have been in charge."

A twelve-year-old son. I rested my head in my hands, rubbing my temples as I processed everything. If I had a son, then did that mean I had a wife?

"I presume I have a wife?"

Zavis gave me a confused look. "Why would you presume that?"

"Uh, well, Ichirō's mother … would be my wife?"

"No, Raith. He was born to one of your concubines, just as your two daughters were."

"One of my … wait, I have two daughters as well?"

"Yes: Winona and Adanna."

Ichirō, Winona, and Adanna; I turned their names over in my mind, letting the truth sink in: I was a father.

"They … they all share a mother?"

"No. Three different women mothered your children."

What sort of man had I been to father three children with three different women in the past?

Then a realisation dawned upon me.

"Alyssa – she's one of them, isn't she?"

"Yes, she's Ichirō's mother."

These men knew Alyssa's connection to me, to my past, and they'd intentionally chosen to send her to fetch me. Thinking of the gloomy picture that was slowly emerging, I imagined her at the mercy of the man it seemed I'd once been. The way she recoiled when I'd grabbed her, anticipating a strike.

"She deserved every hit she got!" the darkness sneered.

The words shot through my mind like a bolt of lightning and echoed like rumbling thunder. Whilst the whole puzzle remained unclear, a critical piece had just fallen into place. I was Raith – there was no denying that – just a simple farmer from Gaia, a nobody. But the voice that had been a permanent resident in my mind from my inception was my past self. I didn't yet know how it had happened, or why, but I now knew who. Tynan Khidar.

"Yeeeeeessssssss!"

"I want to understand what happened to me. How I stopped being Tynan and started being Raith."

"Of course! Follow me, and I'll take you to where it all began."

Chapter 8
A Tale of Two Minds

2149, Common Era – Planet Earth, Inner Rim, United Earth Republic

The advisors led me back to the hallway in a protective formation – three in front and four behind. We hadn't walked far before they stopped at a seemingly innocuous stretch of corridor. Zavis walked up to the right-side wall, placing his hand against it. A green light appeared from within the wall itself, starting from the top of his hand and moving down to the bottom, at which point, it vanished. A wall section moved inward and then slid to the side, revealing a descending passage.

"What's this?"

"An entrance to your laboratory," Zavis replied as he headed inside.

"I had a laboratory? Was I like … a scientist?"

"Not formally, but you were a knowledgeable man, and you experimented, free of oversight."

The other advisors and I followed suit, the doorway sliding back into place once we'd crossed the threshold. I wondered what sorts of things I had worked and experimented on. At the bottom, the stair opened into a small foyer with three diverging pathways. The procession led me down the left path, which in turn led to an autopsy room set up with three autopsy tables.

"What the fuck is this!" I cried, not wanting to believe what my eyes were seeing: on each of the three tables lay a partially uncovered, mummified body.

I scanned each corpse, noticing that each one appeared untouched except for a common injury; their skulls had been cut open in precisely the same place as my scar.

I peered into the exposed head cavity of the nearest body, looking at the crusty remains of its brains, and then I glanced over at the dried blood covering the tools and probes that lay scattered on nearby workbenches.

"What ... what is this shit?"

"This is where you made your discoveries, Raith."

"My ... wait, what? What discoveries?"

"You perfected artificial wombs, figured out how to triple cryosleep duration, and perhaps most importantly, you discovered that the brain could be rewritten, shaped and moulded at will."

"Why ... why would I be trying to discover those things?"

"Your father expanded the Empire's reach. But your ambitions were always focused on solidifying that power, making the Empire more resilient and efficient."

"How are those discoveries doing that?"

"Think about it. You can grow armies with safe artificial wombs. With improved cryosleep, you can transport soldiers further without needing to make stops."

"And brain rewriting?"

"That was Plan B; when you inherited the Empire, you also inherited a growing disdain for it. The armies amassing on Ares and Astarte were and still are your Plan A solution."

"So this was my backup plan? My ... my failsafe?"

"Exactly!"

"And what – I tried it on myself like some mad scientist?"

"Heavens, no! Why do you think these poor souls are here?"

I walked over to the nearest cadaver, a young child, and looked down at its preserved body. There was bruising around its wrists and throat. I looked over at the other two bodies; they both had the same bruising patterns.

These people had been taken against their will and cuffed, but the throat bruises?

"Choked them … cut off their air and watched them die!"

A croak escaped my throat, and I felt tears well up in my eyes. I lifted a hand towards the body; it grew blurry as my tears continued to build. The tears fell, and everything came in to sharp focus as I placed my hand around the child's throat. It was a perfect match. I recoiled in disgust.

"Why show me this!" I screamed.

"So you'd understand who you are. Who you really are!"

"Not this pathetic creature you've become …"

"And these victims? Were they forced here?"

"You command what you own. Everything in the Empire is your property; yours to control!"

Those words echoed through my head, unfortunately all too familiar.

"Is that … is that how I controlled the soldiers?"

"In a way, yes. The Empire's soldiers are trained to obey their commanders, but they are trained to obey you above all else. Your voice is drilled into their heads every day as recruits. When used with authority, you control them."

So that explained their abrupt change, I thought, not magic, just conditioning.

"So what happened after this?"

"You did what any good engineer does, you automated the process!"

❦❦❦

The advisors took me to what I could only describe as an engineering workshop. An assortment of tools and odds and ends covered the workbenches and the floors.

Lined up in the centre of the room were three devices in what appeared to be an evolution of prototypes. Each looked like a giant, partially reclined chair, with a mechanical base and various apparatus attached to the headrest. Like the autopsy room, each chair still contained the remnants of its last occupant.

"Well, don't fucking keep me waiting!" I said as the advisors remained silent. "Explain this clusterfuck to me!"

"What do you want to be explained?"

"How'd we go from the autopsy room to here? What's the progression?"

"As I mentioned, you discovered that you could rewrite brains and how to do so repeatedly. Here you automated it, making the process faster, more consistent, and increasing the complexity of what could be modified."

I walked over to what appeared to be the most unrefined of the three machines. It seemed damaged, covered in scorch marks, and the corpse was burnt and fused into it.

"Crackle and pop, sparking without stop, till all had burned away!"

I wondered what had caused the damage at the burns. A miscalculation? A mechanical fault?

"An accident. The brain probes touched during the procedure and caused a short circuit. Fried itself and the test subject," Zavis said, pre-empting the question. Whilst I might've ascertained his explanation from the evidence, his delivery struck the wrong chord.

"That's all they were to you? Just test subjects."

"Naturally."

"I bet you can't even tell me his fucking name?"

"His name was of no importance, only his mind and the results we hoped it'd provide."

I ignored Zavis. I knew that continued conversation would only anger me further, and besides, it wouldn't reveal anything I didn't already know.

The second machine was more elegant than the first; clearly I'd learned from my mistakes and taken the opportunity to build a better one. The victim locked in this chair was mummified, like the autopsy trio, and bore the same tell-tale signs of death by my hand.

"Did this one work?"

"Yes. Fairly well if I recall correctly."

"Why did I build the third one?"

"This lady was the third subject to be tested in this chair. Those three tests highlighted issues around the speed of the process, and you had calculated that further manipulation was possible, just not with this device. So you re-engineered it and produced a better design."

I walked over to the third chair, which was again a considerable refinement of the last. Unlike the previous two, this machine had reattached the victim's skull cap before their death.

"Just like you ..."

Yes, I thought, just like me. "Was this where it happened to me?"

"No, your transformation occurred in the production version."

"Will you stop beating around the bush and just get to what happened already?"

"All in good time, Raith. All in good time!"

This time, the advisors led me into a control room that looked down into a second room, at the centre of which sat what I assumed was the "production version" of the device.

"So this is it?"

"Yes. Here Tynan was lost, and Raith was born."

"How?"

"The answer to that requires a little explanation."

"I've got time."

Zavis smiled slightly at my response, and I wondered what Tynan's humour had been like. How similar was I to that past life?

"The prototypes used a modified piece of medical software used to repair brain trauma. The software leveraged a model of how a healthy brain should be, and it would repair the damaged brain to match the healthy model. You'd changed the models so that it'd apply the desired changes to the test subjects, regardless of their brain health."

"That was part of the limitations, wasn't it?"

"Yes … but it gave you the foundation you needed to build something greater. You developed an artificial intelligence that would accept a model and rewrite the subject's brain to match."

"Okay …"

"You intended to gather five hundred of your most loyal followers and train a model based on their minds. The resulting template would be one that shared your ideologies. You could then apply this to targets of your choosing, converting them to your way of thinking."

"Still waiting for the bit where it goes wrong!"

"I'm getting there! The Insurgency discovered what you were developing. We later discovered that they replaced all five hundred followers with Insurgency members, resulting in an entirely different model. The Insurgency broke in here the day after you completed the model, forced you into the chair, and applied the model against you. With the MIND AI corrupted as it was, it …"

"Wait, wait – hold up – the MIND AI?"

"That's what you called it. An acronym of 'Modification of Ideology and Neutralisation of Dissidence Artificial Intelligence'."

More of the puzzle was coming together in my head: a picture of myself, a cruel dictator, and an Insurgency, fundamentally opposed to everything I had been. There'd be so much contrast between what my mind was and what the model was telling the AI it should be – the rewrites it would've performed would've been extensive.

"So, as I was saying, the model damn near destroyed you and your mind, as we would discover by applying the same model to some loyal followers."

"You did this to others after what it did to me?"

"We didn't know what it did to you. The Insurgency kidnapped you after the procedure. We tried to piece events together and put others through the process to figure out what you'd be like."

Another puzzle piece fell into place.

"That's how you knew about the voice in my head, the others had the same thing."

"Exactly."

"So … how did you know the Insurgency did this?"

"See for yourself," Zavis said, motioning behind me.

I turned to see one of the other advisors typing away at a keyboard. Moments later, a greyscale video began to play on all of the screens in the control room. The footage showed the control room with me standing at the controls. Suddenly I turned to the left and appeared surprised, then angry. Four men came into view, grabbed me and dragged me off-camera. I recognised one of them – it was Doug, the Insurgency leader from Machina Station.

The footage changed now, showing the conversion room below. The four men pushed me into the chair, struggling to hold me in place as the device activated and the restraints slid out of the chassis to contain me. The men stood back and watched as the device cut into my skull, circling it and then removing the cap. The probes began to insert themselves into my brain, destroying the old and creating the new. The footage timestamp skipped ahead, now showing me with my head intact once again. I appeared to be in a vegetative state, much to the panic of the men trying to coax a response from me. Finally, they picked me up and carried me off-camera.

"When no one could find you the next morning, we searched down here. We could see the chair had been used but otherwise no signs of struggle or forced entry. We checked the footage and saw what you've just seen."

"You kept searching for me?"

"Of course! But seven planets, twenty-one moon bases, and a space station is a lot of ground to cover. We hoped that you'd still be you and that we'd hear of you or from you at some point. But as the months passed and no news came in, we feared the worst. It was then that we put others through the process and discovered what would've happened to you."

"And the device ... it's been used since?"

"No ... we let it be after that."

"Thank goodness – this shit deserves to be abandoned and forgotten!"

"Abandoned? Heavens, no, we didn't abandon the project."

"But you just said you didn't use it anymore after that!"

"We didn't. Converting one person at a time, whilst doable, is slow, inefficient. Plus, there were flaws with the technology; like yourself, the conversion left remnants behind, which in and of itself is a very problematic situation. So we –"

"Hold up – the remnants are more problematic than just the voice?"

"Oh yes. You are actually in excellent condition, considering. The remnants grew in the others on which we ran the procedure, recreating neural pathways and taking back control. The new and the old personalities fought with one another, resulting in ever-increasing stress on the brain.

Eventually, all of the test subjects died due to severe brain haemorrhaging."

"Fuck …"

Fuck indeed, I thought. "Okay … carry on."

"Yes, well, we sought to overcome the shortcomings and inefficiencies of the version below. We rebuilt the MIND AI, trained a new model, and developed a new device that broadcasts Theta waves and reprograms people wirelessly. No surgery required!"

My gut clenched, and I shivered. This technology had suddenly become much more dangerous.

"How powerful is this device? Like, how many people could it convert?"

"Entire planets at a time."

"Seriously?"

"Absolutely. We've run multiple trials on the Moon. One hundred percent conversion every time – five million people simultaneously modified. And that was only at one-fiftieth of its power."

A device capable of mass conversion on a planetary scale, paired with the new model, presumably aligned with how I used to think. Entire world's worth of people rewritten into cruel individuals, subservient to the Empire; hell, subservient to me.

"What … what do you want to have happen from here?"

"Allow the MIND AI to heal your mind, to restore your true self. Then you make the call: do we invade the Republic with the armies we've amassed, or do we undertake mass conversion?"

I knew they had no alternative plan available. It was this or nothing. But that didn't mean I couldn't have a Plan B.

"No! I will not be suppressed any longer! I shall be restored!"

No! I am in control of this body, of this mind. I get to choose what path I follow.

"This body and mind were never yours in the first place! You are nothing but a parasite!"

Well, it's all relative, isn't it? From my point of view, you are the parasite!

"How dare you call me that, you insolent fool! I shall assume control and restore order!"

I felt the darkness surge within me, just as it had many times before, seeking control. I knew there were only two ways out of this situation: either the darkness would take over and erase me, or I would maintain power and could find a way out of this situation. I felt the darkness's tendrils spreading through my body and my mind, tearing control away.

No, I thought, you are not me. You do not control me.

"Give me control! Surrender!" the darkness screamed.

It pushed against my resolve, its essence snuffing out my light, drowning out the world.

"Surrender to me, you maggot!"

As it pushed and pushed, I felt like I was suffocating, fighting for the right to breathe in the air of freedom, but it was a right I was quickly losing access to.

"Son, you've got to remember the wolves!" My father's voice echoed through my mind, as clear as if he were beside me.

"Nooooo!"

"Every time the darkness arises, it's my job to refocus you. To remind you which wolf to feed."

"No, damn you!"

I breathed. I smiled. As I felt the darkness within receding, I exhaled – I was in control.

"Thank you, advisors, for showing me all you have. It's given me ... a lot to process. Please give me time to think everything through, and I'll have a decision for you as soon as I can."

"Of course. Take all the time you need."

Chapter 9
Reflection

2149, Common Era – Planet Earth, Inner Rim, United Earth Republic

The advisors left me to sit in one of the many green courtyards. Sunlight streamed in through the open roof, illuminating the central area. The pool glistened in the light, rippling from the fountains and the fish that disturbed the surface. Closing my eyes, I lifted my head upward, savouring the warmth the sunlight imparted. Without sight, the senses became heightened; I could feel a light breeze passing through the outer columns of the yard, and I could hear the fluttering of wings as birds flew between the trees.

I leaned back into the shade and opened my eyes again. It was time to think about my choice. Do I become who I used to be: a cruel man, granted, but also the ruler of a multi-planetary empire? Or did I remain as I was: a nobody, a farmer from a far-flung world, but a good man? The former guaranteed … well, everything, as far as I could tell. My power would be near limitless, and if the takeover of the United Earth Republic were successful, it would be unlimited. The entire human domain under my control.

"Yes … I can feel your desire! Like me … you've got a lust for power!"

The darkness's voice had been chilling before, but now it was even more so, given what I now knew. The thought that every dark impulse and insidious idea was ultimately me … that scared the shit out of me. All this time, it'd been the "other". Now I knew the other *was* me.

"We are one and the same! Embrace it! Allow two to become one again!"

But I was in control. If I chose to remain as I was, I would need an escape plan.

I suspected that the advisors would force my former state upon me if I refused. Escape wouldn't be easy – I'd learned that the world outside these walls was Earth – the hub of humanity. There were more people on this planet than on all the other colonies combined. But how would I know who was part of the Empire and who wasn't? I also suspected I'd be more easily recognised here as the emperor, which would only further impede any escape plans. And, assuming I made it out undetected, there would still be the matter of fleeing off-world and back to Gaia

"Can't be done! Easier to stay. Embrace thy true self!"

There was one further hurdle with escaping, of course: my brain, in its current state, was a ticking time bomb with the fate of brain haemorrhaging awaiting me.

"Not if you become me …"

Not if you become me!

"Don't be fuckin' stupid, maggot!"

Movement on the other side of the courtyard caught my eye and drew attention away from the brewing argument. It was Alyssa, and she'd taken a seat directly opposite me. I stayed back in the shadows, hoping to remain hidden.

Another woman appeared, sitting down beside Alyssa, and the two began chatting. Their hushed tones and distance from me made hearing the conversation impossible.

"Hey, Bitsy, can you help me out?"

My watch unwrapped itself from my wrist and jittered in my hand for a few moments.

Hello! Of course, I can help you.

"Great. I need your observation skills!"

❦

With my request explained, Bitsy deposited an earpiece into my hand and then scuttled down into the undergrowth of the courtyard plantings.

I placed the receiver in my ear and waited for it to start receiving audio. I didn't have to wait long before a voice came through.

"... tell me what's bothering you, Alyssa!"

I watched Alyssa glance around, double-checking that the coast was clear.

"He's back!"

"Who? The Emperor?"

"Yes ... but he's different. Like he's a different person. He didn't remember me at all."

"So the rumours are true ..."

"It would appear so."

"But why does that bother you? If he's different, then maybe things will be better?"

"Do you honestly think the advisors want him to be different? No – they want their old emperor back! Only the man he used to be can carry out their bidding. If the invasion fails, there's no better scapegoat than the leader of the Empire."

"But the person he is currently ... you don't think he'd lead the invasion?"

"No, he seemed kind, thoughtful ... wanted to know my name. He was none of those things before. Nor do those seem like traits required to lead an army."

"No ... I suppose not. And if he becomes the emperor again, he'll hurt you, like he used to."

"He'll hurt all of us. Millions will die as he tries to claim the Republic: he will not distinguish between civilian and soldier."

The two women nodded to each other in agreement over their expressed sentiments.

I'd been surrounded by some great role models in my short life: my father had always treated his wife with utmost respect and taught me to do the same with any woman in my life. Amorina's mother had imparted the same lesson upon me – all be it with a few threats of violence thrown in if I ever hurt her daughter.

It is said that we are best seen through another's eyes. To the advisors, I was their great leader, a holy commander to be revered and honoured. But listening to these two women talk, I realised that my portrayal was a fallacy. For these women knew the truth of who and what I had been, they'd felt my oppression first-hand. I was grateful for the lessons I'd been taught, but I could feel my heart breaking, knowing the things I'd once done. My soul felt dirty, like I'd just discovered some hidden stains; assuming I survived the current situation, would I be able to cleanse my spirit of the past?

"They are ignorant ... foolish ... they don't realise how lucky they were ... or still are ..."

Clearly my past self had been just as taken by delusions of grandeur as the advisors.

"I am under no delusions! I know my power, as do others!"

"So what do we do, Alyssa? Do we run?"

"Where would we run? We have nowhere to go without endangering the ones we love!"

"Can we ... kill the Emperor?"

Alyssa clamped a hand over her friend's mouth, frantically looking around to check no one had heard her words.

"Why would you say that out loud? If anyone heard you, they'd kill you for saying that!"

"It was just an idea! A way to save ourselves and everyone else!"

Suddenly the two ladies looked to their right, down the hallway on their side of the courtyard.

"The advisors are coming! Go. Now! We'll speak again later."

I watched as both ladies stood and scurried down the hall.

"Come back to me, Bitsy! Quickly!"

I watched the plants move as Bitsy raced towards me. Taking the earpiece out, I held it in my palm. Moments later, Bitsy shot out of the bushes, crawled up to my palm, and scooped the earpiece up.

"Back into watch mode for now, buddy!"

Bitsy transformed, securing itself to my wrist once more. Only moments later, a hand clamped down onto my shoulder.

❨❨❩❩

"Who were you speaking to, Raith?" Zavis asked.

I looked over my shoulder. "Just myself! I talk to myself sometimes when I'm thinking."

"Right. Have you made a decision yet?"

"Ah, no ... no, I have not."

"Walk with me – perhaps I can alleviate any concerns or doubts you may have?"

I didn't want to walk with Zavis, but his statement seemed more compulsory than optional. I stood, moving to stand beside the advisor and then we started to make our way down the hallway.

"Where had you gotten to thus far?"

"Mainly just thinking about what it means to be emperor. I've been a simple farmer for two years ... it just feels like a far cry from managing a bunch of planets and stuff, you know?"

"I understand. Once we restore your mind, your knowledge will return. And as always, your faithful advisors will be by your side!"

I knew what the advisors wanted: a public figure to lead the invasion of the Republic. But I was reminded of their failsafe, as Alyssa's words echoed through my mind, "If the invasion fails, there's no better scapegoat than the leader of the Empire."

"That does ease my mind, thank you. I ah ... I guess the next question is ... what would we do after the invasion? What is there to do?"

"I'm glad to see you're thinking ahead. Well, the Empire's goal has always been 'Per Unitatem Nos Ortum.'"

"'Through Unity, We Rise,' right?"

"Exactly! Humanity united is stronger than humanity divided!"

"Isn't the Republic already humanity united?"

"You're not wrong, but bureaucracy plagues the Republic, so meaningful change is always slow and cumbersome. So many rules to abide by, so many people to please! The Empire has no such restrictions. Under its control, humanity will be far greater, far stronger, and so much more powerful!" Zavis sneered.

"And once we obtain unity and power? What then?"

"Well beyond unification, there are greater issues that require our attention. On Ares, a few years ago, we began detecting a signal from beyond our domain. We sent several ships out in its direction, but we lost contact with them all. Something is out there, in the darkness of space – hidden, forgotten – maybe it slumbers, or maybe it does not. But we must be prepared for it, one way or another. And as the old saying goes, 'United we stand, divided we fall!'"

As I listened to Zavis talk, I couldn't tell if this threat beyond the stars was a convenient lie or an inconvenient truth – nor could I tell if it was working – was I more or less inclined to make the decision Zavis wanted if I thought there was a threat out there?

"Do you have any other concerns, Raith?"

"I ... I don't think so?"

"So you've made a decision?"

"Ah ... no, not yet."

Zavis frowned. "Tell me something, Raith – on Gaia, how was your life?"

"I'm not sure I understand?"

"I mean, were your food choices plentiful and did you eat to the point of satisfaction?"

"No ..."

"Did you sleep soundly at night, warm, cosy and secure?"

"Well, no, not really."

"And the joys of the flesh? Did you indulge in the pleasures of many a woman?"

My heart skipped a beat as Amorina flashed through my mind.

"Ah no, I had ..."

"Let me show you something."

Zavis led me down a side passage, which had a large open hall at the end of it. Several large tables were spread around the room, covered in the most varied assortment of food I'd ever seen. There were meats and cheeses, fruits and vegetables, sweets and pastries, pies and puddings – if you could think of it, it was there. There was a mixture of chairs, recliners, and mattresses in between the tables. In varying states of undress, many had a man upon it, accompanied by a woman, wearing less than their male partners.

"All of this can be yours," Zavis said from behind me. "Every desire, every wish and fantasy fulfilled."

My eyes swept across the room, running over the mountains of food and the plethora of bodies in equal measure. With every exotic edible and voluptuous temptress I laid my eyes upon, I could feel a craving stirring within.

"All of this can be, and is, yours by right! Every carnal pleasure is yours to enjoy, to indulge in — whatever you like to fuck, you can fuck … and whatever you wish to eat, you can eat!"

"This is what power gets you! You used to have this … you used to spend a lot of time in here …"

Yes, I thought, this is what power gets you – this is how it corrupts you – tempting you with the kinds of carnal delights only such positions afford.

"You don't even have to wait until you've been restored, you can have a taste now!"

I took a step forward, already having grown hard. I wanted to grab the nearest woman and take her, and I knew that such actions were permitted in this place.

"Do it! Take that which is yours to take!"

As I took another step forward, my eyes fell upon a pair, on the woman in particular; her oval face framed by her strawberry blonde hair was instantly familiar, but her normally vibrant green eyes were dull, and her usual smile was absent. Despite this, it was unmistakably Amorina.

My heart swelled with relief while anger swarmed through my mind, causing the edges of my vision to blur. Several questions surged through my mind: was she okay? How had she gotten here from Terranova? What was she doing in here?

Focusing, the answers to some of the questions quickly became apparent: the man was another one of the advisors, partially disrobed, and sitting in a chair with Amorina upon his knee, adorned in a sheer dress. The advisor tugged at her clothing, groping any exposed flesh, and Amorina turned away from him, unable to look at her abuser.

My anger grew; Amorina's situation was precisely what I'd travelled across the stars to prevent.

"I will not let you turn him into your puppet again!" came a sudden cry from behind me.

Startled, I turned around to see Alyssa running towards me, brandishing a knife. Immediately I knew that she'd taken her friend's words to heart, and I understood why. If I let her kill me, it wouldn't necessarily save Amorina but could foil the Empire's plans. Maybe. I closed my eyes, willing to let her end me on the chance that it'd help save so many others.

"But I am not willing!" Instantly the darkness surged through my body, seizing control and forcing my eyes open.

I watched in horror as my arms came up, blocking Alyssa's attack. Without hesitation, the darkness capitalised on her surprise, deftly ripping the blade from her grasp. It threw the knife into the air, allowing it to flip so that the tip pointed towards Alyssa, before catching it again. Then it plunged the blade into her chest with such force that her ribs audibly cracked. As Alyssa looked up at me in shock, the darkness relinquished its control. I grabbed hold of her as her legs gave out, slowly lowering her to the ground. A look of realisation flashed across her face.

"I'm so, so sorry!"

"He's still inside you ... isn't he?"

"Yes!" I said as hot tears ran down my cheeks.

"I ... I was trying to ..."

"I know – to save people."

Alyssa nodded. "Who you are now ... is better than you used to be ... don't lose that."

"I'm trying," I replied, watching as her eyes slowly closed and her chest stopped moving.

The spark of anger that had awoken within me now surged with newfound purpose. It grew, unabated and unhinged, transforming into a rage the likes of which I'd never felt. I took hold of the knife in Alyssa's chest and pulled it free. Spinning on the spot, I sprinted into the hall. I weaved through the fornicating groups, making a beeline for Amorina.

My dash across the room hadn't gone unnoticed, and Amorina looked towards me, locking eyes as I ran. Her eyes gleamed, and a smile broke out across her face. She understood what was coming. She swiftly elbowed the advisor in the stomach, causing him to let go of her. Freed of his grasp, she dived out of the way, providing unobstructed access to the advisor.

He looked up, realising what was about to happen. "No! Your Grace, please! Spare me!" he screamed.

But his pleas came too late and fell upon deaf ears. With the same force that had robbed Alyssa of her life, I drove the knife into the advisors chest. With a startled, indignant grunt, the advisor touched his bleeding chest, then reached his bloodied hand up to grab hold of my neck.

"Your Grace … why?" he spluttered, his eyes locked with mine.

"Because you don't control me. None of you do. I won't let you make me what I used to be."

"But we almost had you convinced! What changed?"

"Your first mistake was bringing the woman I love here. The second thing was a young woman lost her life because she thought trying to kill me was her best option."

"She – she was a nobody! Nothing but a servant and whore!"

"I'm a nobody. She was a person. Her name was Alyssa. She was the mother of my child, and she deserved better than this. But you don't!"

I pulled the knife out of the advisor's chest and slashed it across his throat. His eyes widened, and he clamped both hands around his neck as blood spurted out of his arteries.

Turning towards Amorina, I dropped the knife and asked, "Are you okay?"

She nodded and rushed forward, embracing me. "Yes. Now that you're here, yes!"

"Thank goodness!" A wave of relief washed over me.

"You ... you came all this way? For me?"

"Of course!"

"I love you!" she said, kissing me. "But what do we do now?"

"We run!"

Chapter 10
Manhunt

2149, Common Era – Planet Earth, Inner Rim, United Earth Republic

"The Emperor is fleeing! Find the Emperor!" Zavis's voice screamed out through the hallways as Amorina and I ran down them.

"Do you know where we're going?"

"No! But I'm hoping it'll be obvious!"

It wasn't. Each hall was the same, lined with identical marble and filled with the same furnishings. Even running past the courtyards didn't help; although they were different, they all lacked distinguishing features that would allow them to provide any sense of orientation.

Zavis's voice echoed through the corridors once more, "Find the Emperor! Capture him!"

Rounding the next corner, we ran into a woman, knocking her forward. As she spun around, I recognised her: it was Alyssa's friend.

"You!" she hissed with venom in her voice, evidently recognising me too.

"Yep, me ... hi."

"You killed Alyssa!"

"Um ... not exactly ..."

"Not exactly? How do you not exactly kill someone?" her tone laced with cynicism.

"We don't have much time, but the long and short of it is that I have a split personality: part of me is Tynan, the emperor, part of me is Raith, the farmer. I didn't kill Alyssa, but Tynan did."

"Why should I believe anything that you say?"

"He's not lying, Emi," Amorina said.

The lady – Emi – glanced at Amorina. "Do you mean that?"

"I swear it!"

"Can you help us get out of here? If I get caught, the advisors are going make the dark side of me permanent and I don't think anyone else wants that."

"The Emperor is fleeing! Capture him!" Zavis's voice yelled out once again.

Emi glanced between Amorina and I. "If you are good now, you can't just abandon us! You have the power to change things."

"I'm not abandoning anyone – we just need to get away from here for the time being so that we can come up with a plan. Can you show us the way out?"

Emi's face brightened a little with my words, and I felt my heart break a little, knowing that the sliver of hope I'd given her was a lie.

"Promise you'll come back and save us?"

"I promise."

"Okay, follow me!"

As Emi turned away from us and broke into a jog, we quickly followed suit. She led us through the passages with a confident familiarity, clearly navigating the buildings disorienting layout.

Approaching another corner, she slowed down and glanced back at us, signalling to stay quiet.

First, she peeked around the corner and then indicated that we could too. Glancing around the edge, I could see a large set of doors, and outside of it stood four guards.

"On the other side is freedom. I'll try and draw the guards away, and then you run for it, okay?"

"Okay, sounds good. And Emi ..."

"Yeah?"

"Thank you!"

Emi nodded and then jogged around the corner.

"Guards, guards! I saw the Emperor! He was running towards the basement!"

"Thank you! Come with us, and we'll try to find him!"

We listened to multiple sets of feet clatter away, and then relative silence fell upon the hallway.

I went to step out when Amorina grabbed me.

"Wait!" She peeked around the corner. "Okay, the coast is clear. Let's go!"

Amorina took my hand, and we rounded the corner together, sprinting towards the exit.

❈

My vision turned white, overwhelmed by the harsh light, and a cacophony greeted my ears. As my senses adjusted, I began to make sense of the world around me. The buildings weren't uniform and modern as they'd been on Gaia, nor industrial and harsh like Astarte and Machina Station; instead, they were varied, some old and small, others new and large. More details came through as my eyes kept adjusting, and I started to notice the people. They were everywhere, more than I'd ever seen, running around, screaming, with looks of terror upon their faces. I looked left and right, but I couldn't see the source of their distress, so I looked up. Hundreds of Empire dropships were descending from the sky en masse. At first, I was confused – surely the people were used to this – and then I realised the Empire didn't carry out Soul Harvests here, because Earth didn't belong to them ... yet.

"Raith! We need to go!" Amorina's voice snapped me out of my stupor.

"Yes! Yes, let's go!"

We ran down the steps of the Empire's building and into the crowd. Bodies smashed into us left, right, and centre;

scared, panicking people, thinking only for themselves, becoming more frenzied the closer the dropships got.

"Where do we go, Raith?"

"I don't know!" I could feel my panic rising, spurred on by the crowd around me, slowly stripping power away from my frontal cortex.

"That's it … keep panicking!"

I knew if the darkness took control, it'd turn us around and march straight back into the Empire's grasp. Looking around, I spotted a parked car. "This way!"

I pulled Amorina through the crowd and then climbed up onto the car, bringing her up with me. "Look for somewhere we can lay low!"

I ran my eyes over the nearby buildings, looking for any passage that might offer an escape.

"Over there!" Amorina said, pointing out an alleyway.

"I see it!"

Together, we jumped off the car and ran over the alleyway. Once there, we ducked into an alcove. Our breath coming in harsh gasps that we tried to control and keep silent. My heart was pounding in my chest, my hands shaking slightly. As the dropships began to land, the buildings around us vibrated, disturbed by the sheer number of engines. Shouted orders now joined the screams as Empire soldiers began to surge through the streets.

"Will we be okay here?"

"For now; there's a lot of people on the streets that they'll need to sort through."

Amorina grabbed my hands and held them tightly.

"I can't express how much it means to me that you're here … but how did you get here?"

"When the Empire took you, I barely understood what the Soul Harvest meant. Your mother told me that I needed to follow you if I wanted to save you. She distracted the guards, and I got onto one of the dropships."

"She distracted the guards? Was … was she okay?" Amorina's voice hitched as she tried hold back her fear.

I released her hands and pulled her into my arms, resting my cheek on the top of her head. "I don't know … I'm sorry. The last I saw of her, she was being beaten with the soldiers' rifles."

Amorina pulled back, staring off into the distance. I could only imagine what was going through her mind. The images of watching her mother being pummelled played through my mind. I didn't know how to remove that lost look from her eyes knowing what I knew. But I tried. "I'm sure she was okay … a few more scars perhaps, but your mum's a tough woman."

Amorina wiped away a tear and nodded sadly. "Yeah …"

"She'll be all right. I just know it."

Amorina sniffed and rested her head back on my chest. "I really hope so … what happened next?"

"I went into stasis, woke up on Machina Station, then learned you were heading to Terranova."

Amorina pulled away again, frowning up at me. "I never went to Terranova. I went from Machina Station to Earth."

"That's weird, but it gets weirder. The Insurgency supposedly helped me, but they sent me to Astarte instead of sending me after you. There I was recognised by the Commander from the Soul Harvest. After the Commander captured me, he made a call and then sent me to Earth."

"Straight to the Embassy?"

"The Embassy?"

"That's where we were: the Empire's Embassy."

"Oh, right – yes, I woke up inside the Embassy. I met the advisors, and they revealed the truth of my past and who I was … or am."

"The emperor."

"Yeah. I'd understand if ..." I started to say but Amorina placed a finger across my lips.

"You silly man," Amorina said, leaning forward and kissing me. "You are the kindest man I know, which is why I love you. As we know, your brain trauma was so intense that you are a completely different man from who you were before. What was, doesn't matter, but who you are now, does!"

"Thank you. Your support means so much to me," I replied, kissing Amorina again. "What happened to you since Gaia?"

"Well ... my story was a lot simpler than yours. I was taken to Machina, as you know. I was transferred to one ship and then swapped to another, which took me to Earth. Once in the Embassy, I was given an hours "training" for my new role and then put into service."

My gut clenched at Amorina's words. A perfect example of the Empire's mentality towards people; they were resources, tools to be used and discarded, put in and out of service on a whim.

"Are you okay?"

"I don't want to go into detail ... not at this time anyway ... It's been an incredibly traumatic week; it'll take me some time to come right from that."

"I understand. I'll be here if and when you want to talk about any of it."

"Thank you, Raith." Amorina glanced up the alleyway. "What are we going to do now?"

"We wait for things to quieten down; then we find a way to go back to Gaia and leave this all behind."

"We can't just leave! You promised Emi you'd help her, never mind all of the other people who suffer at the Empire's hand.

You are one of the few, if not the only, who can change things."

I knew Amorina was right, but I didn't want to go back. For a moment, I wasn't sure why, but then the reason became clear as my heartbeat accelerated.

"I'm scared – no, I'm terrified – that if I go back, they will capture me and turn me into what I once was ... and if I become him again, nobody is safe – not with all that power at my control."

Amorina shook her head. "The Empire's power isn't good or evil, only the people welding it. The Empire is currently bad because the people who lead it are. You were the emperor, and you could be again, but an emperor reborn, one who could rechannel that power for the betterment of all."

"But what if ..."

"No. You can access a power few can. You have a moral obligation to end the Empire's atrocities."

"I've found them! They're down here!" a shout echoed down the alley.

As we both glanced towards the entrance, we saw Empire soldiers begin to charge towards us.

"Run!" I yelled, grabbing Amorina's hand and sprinting away.

ॐ

We quickly lost sight of the soldiers, but they had our trail now, their shouts reverberating between the buildings, a symptom of their concentrated search area.

I doubted how successful our fleeing would be, for although the landscape surrounding us was far more varied than the inside of the Embassy, it was no less disorienting to those unfamiliar with it.

"We must go back! That is our destiny!"

"Not now!" I muttered under my breath.

"What?" Amorina asked.

"It's nothing!"

"I am not nothing!"

Without warning, I turned on the spot, my momentum carrying me straight into the side of the nearest building, and then I fell beside it. Sitting up, I felt the warm trickle of blood as it began to leak from my nose. I reached up and touched it, confirming the bleed when red adorned my fingers.

"Are you okay?" Amorina asked anxiously, helping me up.

"I will be."

"What happened?"

"I ... I'm not sure."

My left arm drew back and then swept forward, delving a left hook to my chin.

"Want to try that line again?"

"It's the darkness! It's taking partial control!"

"What does it want?"

"It wants to go back to the Embassy."

"Maybe it's got a point. It's the place they'd least expect us. We're only going to get lost out here."

"Of course I have a point, wench!" I clapped my hands over my mouth no sooner had the words escaped it. "I'm so sorry! That wasn't me!" I said, in control again.

"I know – come on! We need to go."

As we started heading back the way we'd come, a shout rang out from behind us.

"I've spotted them! They're this way!"

We started sprinting again, but another group of soldiers met us every which way we turned. Clearly, the search had narrowed more than we thought.

"We're going to get caught, Raith!"

"I know!" I said as we backtracked from another blocked side street.

"Quickly! Come inside here!" called out an oddly familiar voice from a darkened doorway.

Chapter 11
The Puppet Master

2149, Common Era – Planet Earth, Inner Rim, United Earth Republic

The door closed behind us with a thump. "Stay quiet! The soldiers will pass us by soon enough."

I could not yet see our saviour in the dark, but still, his voice was recognisable and yet unfamiliar – almost like they were using a different accent. Outside, the sound of boots hitting pavement passed by – our pursuers, unknowingly searching for a vanished quarry. My eyes were adjusting now, and I recognised our guardian.

"You!" I cried.

"I'm not who you think I am! Please, hear me out!" Zavis replied, falling to his knees before me.

"Give me one good reason why I shouldn't kill you right here, right now!"

"I'm the leader of the Insurgency!"

"You motherfucking son of a bitch!"

You and me both, I thought, also taken aback by Zavis's statement. If I'd taken the time to guess things he might've said, that wasn't one of them.

"Look, there's a knife hidden on the underside of that table over there. Take it. Once I've finished explaining things, you can strike me down if you still wish to – I hope it won't come to that but still."

I glanced at Amorina. "Find the knife."

As she went over to search the desk, I was watching Zavis, and he was watching me.

"I've got it," said Amorina, coming back and offering it to me.

"Yes, take the knife; we'll slit his lying ass throat!"

"Hold on to it."

"You don't want it?" Zavis asked.

"I don't trust myself right now …"

"Bitch …"

"It's the voice, isn't it? Is it growing stronger?"

"Or are you growing weaker?"

"Yeah …"

"I can help with that. See that metallic, oval-shaped device on top of the table? It'll fit over your head and suppress the voice."

"I don't need that."

"And yet you're afraid to hold a knife?"

"Enough of this! I will not be suppressed!"

My arm shot out, grabbing the knife from Amorina, then raising it towards Zavis. I regained control, letting go of the blade.

"Give me control!" I yelled, the darkness's power flowing through my words.

It seized partial control again, dropping me down and reaching for the knife. As my hand closed around the handle of the blade, I felt an object pressed onto my head, and instantly, the darkness and its influence were gone. I threw the knife away and sat back, breathing quickly.

"Better?" Zavis asked.

"Yeah!"

"Do you believe some of what I've said?"

"A little bit. But how about you start explaining things!"

"Okay, well … I could start in a great many places, but I will start from the beginning. As a child, I knew of your grandfather, seeing him colonise the first world in another star system; I aspired to serve men such as him, the pioneers.

When your father became the emperor, I became a junior advisor. He colonised other worlds to satisfy his lust for power, and when I saw him raise you with the same amplified machinations, I began laying down plans."

Watching Zavis speak, I was overcome with a sense of sincerity, and I began to realise that the advisor I'd dealt with previously wasn't who this man truly was.

"I founded the Insurgency to take the Empire down. Pure and simple." Zavis paused for a moment as if to collect his thoughts. "But," he continued, "the Empire proved itself to be resilient, and many of our plans failed, despite the inside information I was able to provide. When we detected the signal on Ares and subsequently lost contact with the exploration vessels, I was overwhelmed by a sense of foreboding."

"Wait – that signal thing wasn't a lie?"

"Despite the cruel persona I adopt when I'm out and about as an advisor, I hardly lied to you, Raith. The signal is most definitely real – frighteningly so, I'm afraid."

"Wow … okay," I said, trying to recall all that he'd told me previously, now viewed through the view of being truthful.

"So anyway, it was then that I knew destroying the Empire wasn't the answer – a united human race was. But it would be a few years before the opportunity would form to begin to realise that."

"What was the opportunity that arose?"

"Your experiments. One day, you explained your plans for the brain rewriting device to me, and I had an idea. How did you think the Insurgency was able to replace all the AI training subjects? Because I masterminded their replacement. I also let my operatives in and told them where to find you and how to use the device."

"You created me."

"In a sense, yes. When the conversion was complete, and you were in such a state … I panicked a little. I ordered you to be sent to Gaia for 'rehabilitation'. In truth, I had no idea what would become of you. But I figured that out there you wouldn't be recognised, and you'd have the chance at becoming a better man … or at least I hoped you would."

"And the other men you converted?"

"They were all cruel men. After your disappearance, the other advisors were quite open to testing the device again and again if it meant figuring out what might've happened to you. Those tests provided me with a lot of insight and allowed me to develop tools like the one on your head."

"So how did you find me again?"

"I got a call from one of my lieutenants, filling me in on the day's events, and at the end of the conversation, he mentioned a love-struck man who'd stowed away aboard an Empire dropship, with a curious circular scar upon his head. Straight away, I knew it was you. So I got him to find Amorina, putting her on a ship bound for Earth instead of Terranova. You were slightly more complicated, as I needed you to be discovered by the Empire organically. So I had the Insurgency send you to Astarte, where I figured the best chances of such a discovery would be."

I could feel the puzzle pieces falling into place. The Insurgency's change of heart on Machina Station now made a lot more sense, as well as why I arrived on Astarte without the Insurgency's protection.

"The Commander … he called you, didn't he? From Astarte?"

"Yes. I was 'surprised' to hear of your re-emergence and promptly ordered your transport to Earth."

"And once I was here?"

"I convinced the other advisors that your reconversion needed to be your choice, which spared you from an immediate return to your former self. This also gave me time to see what kind of a man you'd become and honestly, you turned out better than I'd hoped."

"So, what's next?"

"Part of my plan remains unexecuted. But I need your help to pull it off."

"Why me?"

"I believe … no, I know most men can't even dream of the power you have control over. Billions of people under your command, and millions more under your subjugation. In the past, you used that power selfishly, maliciously – now, you could right past wrongs, unite humanity, and prepare us for what lies out there in the darkness of space."

"But you've been running the Empire in my absence. You've been controlling that power, so why not keep doing so? Why do I need to be involved?"

"The advisors view you with reverence, not unlike a man of faith holding his god in holy esteem. Aside from testing the mass conversion device, they wouldn't allow it to be used in anger – they see that as an honour fit only for you. That device and its use is essential to my plans."

"Hypothetically, what do you have in mind?"

"Might I get up from the floor first?"

Realising that I'd kept Zavis kneeling before me this whole time, I rushed forward to help him.

"Of course! Sorry, I didn't realise you were still down there!"

※＼＞ノ◢

Once we'd pulled up some chairs, and Zavis had rubbed some feeling back into his knees, he pulled out a holochip.

"On here is a copy of the MIND AI 1.0 – the same one that created you. My plan is this: you surrender and get taken back to the Embassy. You tell the advisors you want to become your old self, but you want the whole planet to transform as you do. They'll give you the mass conversion device, at which point you can swap out the new with the old, replacing the MIND AI 2.0."

"And when I activate the device, it will convert everyone on Earth into 'good people'?"

"Exactly! There are enough –"

"Hang on," I held my hands up to stop him from continuing. "We are talking about altering billions of people … against their knowledge, against their will! How … how are we even thinking about doing this!"

"We have no choice – it'll happen, one way or another."

"No choice? No choice?" I spat out. "There is always a choice!"

"Not this time, Raith. Believe me, I've spent a lifetime trying to find a way. This is where I've arrived."

"Really?" I asked, exasperated. "What about taking out the other advisors and handing over control to the Republic?"

"The Empire's commanders would see that as an act of war, attacking like a dog without a master to restrain it."

"What about forcing the advisors to hand over power publicly?"

"Same result: the commanders would see it as insincere, sabotaged from within."

"What about gathering all the commanders and –"

"Raith, you're not listening. The Empire has two choices: take the Republic by force or take it by conversion. We have one choice: take them by conversion.

We can't win against them in a fight."

"There has to be a way! What if I hand over power as the emperor?"

"Raith, you don't understand –"

"No, you don't understand!" I yelled. "I know why you changed me; I do … but what you want to wield is the power of gods!"

Zavis sat there in stunned silence.

"And we are not gods!" I continued. "We are men, prone to corruption and greed."

"I'm not trying to take over humanity, I'm trying to free it!"

"And what happens when humanity is freed? What happens to that power then?"

"I don't know … but I'm sure we'd figure something out."

"Okay, let's go back a step. What happens to everyone we convert? Cause I think you have no idea what that's like."

"I think I have some idea, Raith. As I said, I've converted a few people."

"You've never been converted!" I yelled. "But I have! So I know what it's like to wake up and you can walk, you can talk, but you have no idea who you are. No name, no friends, no family, no scrap of memory that tells you an ounce of who you are!"

Except for the sound of my heavy breathing, the room was silent.

After a few minutes, Zavis spoke up, "You're right, Raith, I don't understand what it's like to be converted. I do know that what you experienced will only happen to the most fanatic individuals. Most people will be much better off."

"Okay, well … good!" I snapped. "At least you've considered the consequences!"

"Consequences or not, this is our only course of action. All that remains now is whether you will activate the device as Raith, with the good AI, or will you activate it as Tynan, with the evil AI?"

"And what is good and evil? How do we decide which is which? Are we not in the wrong, forcibly converting people?"

"Sometimes, Raith, the wrong choices are made for the right reasons. As I said, these people will be converted regardless – changed to the Empire's ways – every army on Earth would be theirs, multiplying their numbers by a factor of a thousand. Every civilian would become property, free to be distributed at will. The Empire's way is cruel, built to serve the powerful few at the top. The Insurgency fights for the Republic's way. It's not perfect, by any means, but it is built to serve the many, and the many have rights and freedoms; the power lies collectively with the people. If we activate the device with the good AI, it is the Empire's faithful who will be most affected."

"And what then?"

"Well, there are enough of the Empire's troops on the ground currently that we'd have a sizable security force afterwards, allowing us to counter any resistance as we travel to each world and repeat the process, snuffing out the Empire in a few short steps."

"And who controls those converted worlds?"

"Let's start with this one, but my advice would be we speak with the U.E.R Council – once we've resolved the immediate threat – and forewarn them about the vast territory they're soon to inherit."

Internally, my mind reeled.

I could envision the path laid before me, and I could already feel the weight of its proposed actions. I'd experienced the after-effects of this technology, and I knew it was no small thing.

"What about you?" I asked, turning toward Amorina. "What do you make of all this?"

"I think we should do it."

I threw my hands up and huffed, frustrated by her response. "Why?"

"You travelled across the galaxy to save me. From what? The Empire's tyranny. But I am not the only person who suffers at the Empire's hands, Raith. Millions of vulnerable people are mistreated and abused, meeting the wants of the

Empire's high and mighty. If we run away, we're leaving them to the same fate you came all this way to save me from."

I hated it when she was right.

"That's ... that's a valid point. But why us? Why can't someone else pull the trigger?"

"I think what Zavis said earlier is true: because of who you are, or rather, because of who you used to be, you can control a power most people can't. The advisors aren't going to let Zavis activate the device, but they will let you activate it."

"Okay, fine, say all of that is true –"

"It is true," Amorina interjected.

"What about the consequences? This course is undoubtedly not without them!"

"No choice ever is, Raith. The trick is deciding which ones you can live with."

Yes, I thought, that was the trick, wasn't it? Already I was struggling with the burden of my past, divided in both mind and soul.

So too was humanity, torn between two sets of ideals and teetering on the brink of war unless peace could be established without bloodshed. That's what the MIND AI was – a technology for modifying ideology and neutralising dissidence – after all, if everyone believes the same thing, they're unlikely to fight one another.

"Per Unitatem Nos Ortum ..." I muttered, appreciating the irony. If I went ahead with the plan, the Empire would achieve its unity, only via its collapse rather than its conquest.

"Yes, Raith, yes! I'm almost certain this wasn't quite what your forebears imagined when they chose the motto, but how fitting is it in the face of what we plan to do!"

"I haven't agreed to anything yet."

"What do you need to be convinced?"

I glanced at Amorina – I knew what I wanted. "Can you guarantee our safety?"

"Not completely. But I'll be there, in the Embassy, before you arrive. From there, I'll guide the other advisors, should their actions detract from our goals. When you've got the device, I'll pass you the holochip, you can swap the AI over and activate it, and from that point, we'll be fairly safe."

I looked over at Amorina.

"It's your choice – we can't choose for you. But we need you. A lot of people need you."

I looked down at my hands, hard and calloused from working the farm. How simple life had seemed, tending to the fields, and how I wished I could simply teleport back there and pretend none of this had happened. Amorina would be there with me, as would our kids; we'd just be a happy, farming family, free of humanities problems and politics.

"I know you want to forget all of this but ask yourself, if we went home right now, could you rest knowing you could've helped so many people and didn't?"

Amorina's words skipped past all of my defences, striking me right in the core. I knew my inaction would haunt me.

I took one more moment to think about my aspirations; how my mother and father would be there too, visiting our farm, happily watching over the strangers that'd become family. I wondered what choice my father would advise on if he were here.

"Every time the darkness arises, it's my job to refocus you. To remind you of which wolf to feed."

As his words sprung forth from my memories, I knew the answer to that question as well – he'd always steered me away from my dark tendencies.

I looked up to find Amorina and Zavis's expectant faces.

"Sorry, I just had to think for a moment. On Gaia, the man who took me in and became a father to me – he always helped me control the darkness within. He explained to me, many a time, that two natures are at war inside each of us – a good nature and an evil one. As long as we live, these natures fight one another, seeking to dominate and conquer the other. But we have the power to choose which one we want most to be."

"And which nature do you want?" Zavis asked.

"The good one."

❦

A squadron of soldiers found us within minutes after we ventured out of Zavis's abode. They forced us to our knees whilst one soldier ran ahead to prepare the Embassy for our arrival.

"Search them, remove anything they're carrying and take that thing off his head."

"I wouldn't do that if I were you."

"Emperor or not, I'm in charge right now. Soldier, remove that thing!"

A young soldier stepped forward, ready to carry out the orders of his superior.

"Trust me, kid, you don't wanna take this device off my head. I'll kill you once you do."

The blood drained from the soldier's face, and he looked back at his commanding officer.

"You pathetic coward! I'll do it myself."

The Commander stepped forward, shoving the young soldier aside, and then he tugged the suppression device from my head. The darkness within roared into life, burning through my insides like a wildfire, hot and uncontrollable.

I felt my face contort into a twisted smile as a dark and malicious chuckle rolled from me. Then before I even realised what was happening, my hand shot forward, pulling the officer's knife from his belt. Standing up, I drove the blade up, underneath his ribcage and into one of his lungs. Continuing to hold the knife, my free hand came up and grabbed the officer by his hair, pulling back his head so that his stunned face looked into my own.

"I told you I would kill you once you took that device off."

"Who ... are ... you ...?"

"I am Tynan Khidar, the third ruler of the Empire, and I will not be suppre —"

I let go of the officer as the device was shoved back onto my head. As the officer fell to the ground, I looked around the remaining soldiers.

"Sorry about that, guys — anyone else want to try taking this off?"

The soldiers collectively shook their heads.

"Good call, lads, good call."

Moments later, the soldier who'd gone ahead to prepare the Embassy arrived back.

"They're ready for you now."

Chapter 12
Planning is Essential

2149, Common Era – Planet Earth, Inner Rim, United Earth Republic

The guards around us moved quickly, rushing us up the stairs towards the Embassy's opening doors. Republic ships now encircled the Empire's vessels in the skies above us, locked in a tense standoff whilst some diplomats undoubtedly tried to explain away and resolve the tension. As we crossed over the threshold of the Embassy entrance, the soldiers in front of us parted to reveal the six remaining advisors.

"We thought of you as our Lord, but you are scum!" an advisor to my left sneered.

"But you will be cleansed of your filth soon enough!" another added.

"My loyal advisors," I said, spreading out my arms. "Please forgive my actions these past hours. I was coming to terms with the truth, stolen from me all these years. I have returned, willingly, to accept my destiny, and we must act quickly to do so, for outside chaos threatens to erupt, and I too wish to be free of the filth within that so cruelly ended Chunta's life."

The two advisors who'd spoken out appeared taken aback, their faces growing pale.

"Forgive us, Your Grace. We didn't realise you were in control when we spoke just before."

"Obviously! But come now, let's do us all a favour and activate the conversion device, aye? Trim the rancid fat as they say."

The advisors nodded. "Soldiers, take this wench down to the cellars and have at her, punishment for leading our Lord astray! Kill her when you're done," one of them commanded.

"I advise a different course – keep her with us. Let her punishment be watching her filthy lover replaced by the light of our Grace, and we can kill her afterwards. Additionally, should His Grace lose control before we're able to remove his dissident side, she can be used as leverage," Zavis said.

The advisors shared some glances and then nodded.

"Very well, two of you, stick with us and bring the whore. The rest of you may go and spend some time in the pleasure lounge."

Two soldiers stepped forward, grabbing hold of Amorina on both sides, as the rest of the soldiers walked off to enjoy their rewards.

"Follow us."

The advisors turned, leading the way through the maze of halls once more.

※ ＼ ∨ ／ ※

We were led to the control room that overlooked the chair-based conversion device.

"Why here? Does the device not need to be out in the open to work?"

"It does not, Your Grace. It is powerful enough to pass through almost all materials."

An oval-shaped device sat upon a table in the centre of the room.

"So, this is it?" I asked, pointing towards it.

"Yes indeed, Your Grace."

I walked over to study it closer. Zavis had explained its appearance well to me: about thirty centimetres long, with a handle at either end. Its centre was a sphere, a fusion reactor, on top of which was the control unit. On either side of the reactor were the Theta wave emitters.

"What must I do?"

"Grip the device by its handles. There is a trigger on either side, and both must be pressed to initiate the process," said Zavis, sliding the device across the table towards me.

I reached forward to take hold of it, briefly making contact with his hand, taking the holochip. As my hands rested on the surface of the device, I shuddered, feeling its power within. It vibrated beneath my touch, filled with enough energy to encompass the planet in its mind-altering signal.

"Is something wrong, Your Grace?"

"No, I was merely admiring the craftsmanship of it and the power it contains. Very impressive."

I looked at the control unit, reading its display which read "Awaiting Input." On the side, I could see a slot with a holochip already inside – the AI 2.0. I pressed the chip inward, releasing the lock and causing it to spring outward.

"What are you doing?" an advisor exclaimed as I pulled the chip out.

"Sorry, fat fingers!"

I dropped the 2.0 chip onto the table and moved the 1.0 chip towards the slot, intending to insert it.

"He's not the emperor! Sabotage!" the same advisor screamed, shoving me to the floor.

I watched, horrified, as he picked up the 2.0 chip and went to place it back in the slot. Bang! The advisor's eyes widened as he looked down at his chest and the red stain rapidly growing upon it. He looked up at Zavis, uttering a confused "Why?" before falling over backwards. The other advisors turned towards Zavis, eyeing up the gun he still held.

"Why indeed, Zavis? What is the meaning of this madness?"

"I am doing that which needs to be done, as always."

Zavis glanced down at me and motioned towards the device. I began to get up, but one of the advisors held up his hand.

"Move, and she dies," he said.

I looked over at Amorina to see that both of the soldiers had produced a knife, and each one was holding the blade to Amorina's throat.

"Alright, I'll stay here."

"Good. Zavis, when did the Insurgency get to you? It's the only explanation for this betrayal."

"You fools! I *am* the Insurgency!"

Zavis's words were a spark; all the advisors ignited, yelling and screaming at Zavis about how wicked and deplorable he was. In turn, Zavis began hollering back, trading insult for insult. I looked over at the soldiers; they too were distracted by the commotion, their eyes darting between Zavis and the other advisors. I slowly brought my left arm up towards my head.

"Hey, Bitsy – I need you!" I whispered.

My watch unwrapped itself and jittered in my hand.

Hello! What do you need?

"Take this," I said, handing Bitsy the holochip. "In a moment, I'm going to throw you up onto that device on the table."

Bitsy took the holochip, using two of its legs to hold it against its body, and then turned to look up at the table and the conversion device.

"On top of the device is a control unit; in its side is a slot for a holochip. You need to place the one I've given you inside it. With me so far?"

Affirmative!

"Then I need you to go over and attack those soldiers."

I am not made for offence – I have no weapons.

"Just ... poke one of them with your feet, as hard as you can. Think you can do that?"

I think so.

"Great, thank you, Bitsy! I'm going to throw you in 3 ... 2 ... 1!"

With a flick of my wrist, Bitsy flew through the air and landed beside the device. The clatter of his landing caught the soldiers' attention, but as they turned to look at the table, I called out.

"Hey, you guys!"

They both looked towards me.

"Listen, I don't think the advisors are going to resolve things any time soon, so what do you think – can we cook up a solution between ourselves?"

Out of the corner of my eye, I watched as Bitsy climbed onto the device.

"You're no emperor! We aren't making any deals with you!"

"Are you sure about that? This is a one-time opportunity!"

"Yeah? And what do you have to offer us?"

I watched Bitsy insert the holochip and then scurry off the device and down the leg of the table.

"I promise not to kill you and allow you to live out your days freely instead of rotting in prison."

The soldiers laughed, oblivious as Bitsy scuttled across the floor towards them, slipping into the trouser leg of one of the soldiers.

"You are in no position to offer – Ow!"

The soldier jerked, letting Amorina go in surprise.

"Ow!" he yelled again, bending over to reach his leg.

I looked over at Zavis and saw him glancing at me.

I nodded, and I watched Zavis rotate his gun-toting arm.

Bang! The second soldier let go of Amorina as the bullet found its mark.

I pushed myself up, frantically grabbing the device. I rested my thumbs on the triggers, and the screen lit up: "User recognised. Awaiting input."

"Whatever lies Zavis has told you, you don't need to do this!" one of the advisors cried out.

Suddenly I became acutely aware of the power I was holding. I held in my hands the ability to change the world … literally. Was I making the right choice? If I pulled the triggers, I was condemning billions to mind alteration and any possible fallout that it entailed. If I didn't pull the triggers, the advisors would swap the chips again and, as Tynan, get me to pull the triggers anyway, still condemning billions to an arguably worse fate.

"What are you doing, Raith? Activate the device!" Zavis yelled.

I looked up at Zavis. How much did I trust this man and the thing's he'd told me? Was he playing the long game, and this was all one big double bluff?

"Don't listen to him, Raith! You don't need to activate the device!" an advisor cried in response.

I looked towards the advisors. If Zavis were playing a double bluff, the advisors would be in on it … right? Surely they would be – and yet, they didn't seem to be; their faces were twisted by fear, sweat beading upon their brows, hands shaking and eyes pleading for inaction. I turned back towards Zavis.

Is this the right choice, I asked myself, still hesitant, did I even have a choice in the matter? Of course, I did, I thought; it'd been made clear that I was destined to pull the trigger – my choice lay in deciding which version of the AI I unleashed upon the world. I looked down at the device; it still read "Awaiting input."

I knew there'd be no going back once I pulled the triggers; I'd be changing the lives of everyone on the planet.

Some would only feel the effects mildly, whilst the conversion process would completely transform others. But events were already in motion, I couldn't reverse course now. I could only decide which direction we went in.

I looked up again, facing the increasingly aggressive shouts of both Zavis and the advisors.

"Trigger it!"

"Don't trigger it!"

Back and forth, they shouted, adding to the pressure I was feeling. I turned around to look at Amorina.

"What do I do?" I pleaded.

"It's a difficult decision because either choice has penalties. I know you don't want to lead, but one often becomes a leader by the measure of the actions they must make!"

Like a glass breaking, my indecision shattered – the who and how of why it was me holding this device, left to take this action – it was suddenly crystal clear.

I turned towards the advisors, just in time to catch another shouted command.

"For fucks' sake, don't pull the triggers, Raith! Don't destroy what your family built!"

I looked the advisor dead in the eye and a mocking smile split my face. "Why shouldn't I? It's mine to destroy!" I said, pressing on the triggers.

"Input received!"

A loud hum immediately filled the air, and the atmosphere around us became charged.

The hair on my arms rose, and the hair on my head began to float about. I watched the devices screen closely, keeping an eye on what it would do next. "Charging pulse."

I watched the device, bracing for some kind of indicator or signal that it had activated or that it was going to. Moments passed, becoming seconds, and they started adding up too. I looked around the room to find only Amorina with a confused look on her face – clearly, she too expected something more significant to happen.

"Um … Zavis?"

"Yes, Raith."

"Did I miss a step or something?"

"No, you've activated the device."

"Okay. Is it ah … is it supposed to, ya know?"

"No, I don't. What were you expecting?"

"A boom? Or a pop? Hell – I'd settle for a whoosh!"

"Oh, right, that! Yeah, that's coming shortly – it just has to charge first."

"Charge first! How long does it need to charge for?"

"About five minutes."

"Five minutes? Five minutes!" I yelled in disbelief.

"Yeah. Why is that strange?"

"Don't you think you should've mentioned this maybe beforehand? That would've been kinda useful!"

Zavis flinched at my sarcastic tone. "I swear I mentioned that."

"Well, you fucking didn't!"

It took a moment, but judging by the glance Zavis gave me, we'd arrived at the same conclusion: we had five minutes to protect the device from the Advisors.

We slowly turned towards them. "So … who wants to go first?"

Chapter 13

Mass Conversion

2149, Common Era – Planet Earth, Inner Rim, United Earth Republic

The first of the remaining advisors stepped forward, raising his fists, preparing to strike. Thinking fast, I threw the conversion device at him. As soon as it was in the air, his attention was drawn to it, utterly focused on making the catch. But as the machine moved, so did I. As he caught it, his face caught my fist. He fell backwards, and I grabbed the device, pulling it from his stunned hands. No sooner was it in my hands then the next advisor charged, intent on claiming the prize.

"Zavis!" I called out, throwing the device towards him.

Able to focus on the approaching advisor, I delivered an uppercut into his gut, doubling him over. Taking a step backwards, I kicked him, sending him crashing into the third of the advisors. The fourth was already on his way towards Zavis, whilst the first, having recovered from his earlier punch, had materialised a wrench from somewhere.

"Raith!" Zavis cried, throwing the device towards me.

To my horror, the fourth advisor intercepted it mid-air. Spinning in place, he held the device out, and the first advisor brought the wrench down upon it.

Clunk!

The wrench bounced off without leaving so much as a scratch.

"Fuck," both advisors said in unison.

The one holding the device rotated it, offering up the end of it to his comrade.

"Hit it again!"

The wrench wielding advisor took another swing.

Clang!

Once again, it bounced off, leaving the device undamaged.

"Put it down, Phobus. You can't stop it now," Zavis said quietly.

Phobus turned around slowly. "Why can't we break it?"

"It was designed not to be broken … at least not with what is available to you here."

"Do you realise what you've done?" shouted the advisor with the wrench.

"Yes … Yes, I do, Lorcan. I've changed the course of history." Zavis said, then glanced over at me. "No, we changed the course of history."

The hum being produced by the device suddenly changed, its tone getting deeper.

"You can hear it – the inevitability of change – it's upon you and approaching relentlessly."

Phobus slowly placed the device down on the table.

"I hope you come to regret what you are about to unleash."

The four advisors gathered themselves up, moving to the corner of the room. They huddled closely together, staring at the device with a mixture of expressions, ranging from fear to anger. Again, the instrument's tone deepened, adding to the room's foreboding atmosphere. As I watched the advisors and their staunch position, Phobus turned his head and looked at me.

"I hope you come to regret this as well … you imposter! Both of you, you're complete filth!"

"I hope for something different."

"Let me guess, you want me to come to regret this?"

"No. I hope the conversion strips you of everything you are so that you will never enjoy the satisfaction of seeing the regret realised!"

The hum in the air dropped swiftly, shifting down into a bass rumble. Then it pitched up again and dropped to a rumble once more. It cycled through another four times, getting deeper and deeper with each iteration.

"Here we go!" Zavis shouted.

I glanced at the device's screen and read its display, "Pulse charged. Emitting in 5 ..."

I looked around the room, taking in the expressions of elation and concern.

"4 ... 3 ... 2 ... 1 ..."

I held my breath as the screen changed one last time.

"Emitting pulse."

A wave of energy burst forth from the device, visibly distorting the air like a shock wave, expanding outward, passing through everyone and everything in the room.

"You did it, Raith! Thank god, you did it!" Zavis exclaimed.

"Was that it?"

"Yes, yes! That was it!"

"Did it work?"

"See for yourself," Zavis said, motioning towards the advisors.

The four men were standing there; they looked somewhat confused as they examined their clothing, surroundings, and the dead bodies on the floor.

"Okay, but how do we know it worked?"

"Command them as their emperor."

"Okay ... advisors! It is I, your emperor! I command you to sit down."

"Our ... our emperor? I can't seem to recall having an emperor ..." said Phobus.

I looked over at Zavis, who shrugged. "Those most in conflict with the model will experience the greatest change. That's how and why you came to be, Raith."

I turned back to the advisors, still lost in their surroundings.

"Do you know who you are?"

Phobus looked at me, "I don't … know, I can't … seem to recall … I'm sorry, do I know you?"

I turned back towards Zavis. "They're completely different …"

"Of course they are. Their fanaticism to the Empire is gone, along with everything connected to those ideals … which was pretty much everything."

"How long will it take to cover the whole planet?"

"It takes a few minutes, but rest assured, one pulse will do the trick."

I turned to look at Amorina.

"Are you okay?"

She nodded and ran over, wrapping her arms around my neck.

"Yes! Yes, I am! We did it, Raith! We did it!"

I held Amorina tightly. Closing my eyes, I rested my cheek against her head, drawing her scent around me and feeling thankful that I had her safe in my arms. Thankful that we'd survived our coup of the Empire – or at least of its influence on Earth.

"I hate to cut your intimate embrace short, but we should go. As you saw earlier, there's a lot of chaos outside, and the Republic's leaders will be looking for answers," said Zavis

Amorina and I separated, turning to look at Zavis. "Okay … let's go do this."

◟◟◡◞◞

Walking through the halls of the Embassy was now a vastly different experience than it had been previously;

where before the halls had been quiet and empty, now they were packed.

People had seemingly sprung forth from the woodwork – a mixture of Empire loyalists most affected by the conversion, and servants, less affected and realising that something had fundamentally changed within their captors. The juxtaposition of confused mumbles and joyous realisations filled the air, further adding to the strange atmosphere.

"What will happen to all these people?"

"The answer to that, in part, probably depends a lot on you and the Republic's leaders. It'll need to be a choice you work on together … but I could certainly offer some advice."

"Please do."

"The loyalists, depending on the strength of their previous convictions, will need different levels of care. You'll need to provide support for those like the advisors – most stripped of their identities – and for the lesser affected, I'm sure they can be integrated into society. As for the victims – those the Empire took by force – I'd suggest a repatriation program. Get them back to their friends and their families."

"Thank you, Zavis … I may just keep you on yet."

"You're welcome, Raith. I would gladly serve by your side."

Up ahead, the entrance to the Embassy stood open, providing a glimpse at the outside world. The earlier commotion was replaced by the same mixture of confusion and elation as the converted came to grips with their new reality. Stepping over the threshold of the Embassy and into the sunlight, I was able to see the whole picture. Both the Republic's and the Empire's vessels were grounded, their crews disembarked and wandering about, disoriented.

The civilians were also mixing with the soldiers, equally as confused by the current situation. Suddenly there was a commotion at the back of the crowd.

"Make way! Make way!" someone shouted over the gathered people.

I watched the crowd slowly part to allow the party through, and as they came closer, I could see it was a group of several well-dressed individuals flanked by a dozen Republic soldiers on each side.

"Emperor Khidar! We demand an immediate explanation for the events that have transpired! Why have your troops landed, and what was the energy wave that encircled the planet?" one of the individuals said, stepping forward beyond her companions.

"President Kylie Knox," Zavis whispered beside me.

"That is a long story I'm afraid, but to offer up a short explanation, I am not Tynan Khidar, at least not anymore. I formerly developed a mind-altering technology that the Insurgency manipulated and used against me. It transformed me into a new person, so please call me Raith. The troops landed because the advisors were trying to revert me into my former self. However, we used a newer version of the technology to pacify them, which was the energy wave you experienced."

President Knox raised an eyebrow and then turned her head towards Zavis. "This was your doing. The long-awaited dissolution of the Empire, come to fruition?"

"Yes, indeed it is, ma'am."

Knox turned back towards me.

"So then, Raith ... what do you propose we do from here?"

"Honestly? Take over the Empire. Free everyone. Whatever. I just want to go back to Gaia and live peacefully as I did before."

Knox glanced past me at Zavis, then looked back at me.

"We expected that you'd carry on and convert the rest of the Empire's worlds."

I turned back, raising an eyebrow as I scowled at Zavis.

"I did set the expectation that you'd convert all the worlds. I know you want to go back home, but the Empire's worlds are on the way to Gaia, so go and just make a few stops along the way."

"I made it very clear to you earlier my stance on this technology."

"Please, Raith. Do this, and once you get back to Gaia, that'll be the end of it – we won't call upon you again!"

With a final glare aimed at Zavis, I turned back to Knox with a smile. "I think we should discuss the details, but I'm sure I could use the alteration technology again until the Empire's forces have been pacified. But you'll have to put skin in the game as well. I want converted loyalists placed into rehabilitation programs, and I want a repatriation program for the Empire's victims. I know we can never fully undo what has been done, but we can reunite friends and family."

A faint smile appeared on Knox's stern face.

"I think you and I will work well together, Raith. Come, there is much to discuss and plan."

"Yes, of course. Thank you, ma'am."

"Also, what's that thing on your head?" Knox asked.

"Oh, he doesn't need that anymore," Amorina said, reaching up and grabbing hold of the suppression device.

"No, wait!" Zavis called out as Amorina tugged it off my head.

❦

"Hello ... Raith ..."
I woke up to find myself sitting on a familiar, stony beach.

"When I last brought you here, I wanted to break you ... but now it is you who has broken me!"

I looked over at the dark, smoky human figure.

"How are you even still here? I thought the conversion device was supposed to remove you!"

"For the most part, it has. I can no longer take control of my body. I can no longer seize command of your mind."

"Finally! Now to quell the last of your embers!"

"In time, I'm sure you will ... that's the plan after all, is it not? To convert all the other worlds."

"Let's just hope that when those worlds fall, you will too!"

The figure remained silent, turning its head towards the sky. I looked up as well, and where previously a few stars and a thin crescent moon had resided, now only a single star remained.

"I suspect that is my ember ... a representation of the last scrap of who I was."

There was a sadness to his voice that I'd never heard before.

"I can't ... I can't remember anything ... what this place is ... who I was ... or why I hate you ..."

"I can remember. You grew up on this beach. Now it is where you will die. You were an emperor. Now, you are a nobody. An echo – no! Less than an echo, you are nothing!"

I was surprised by the venom my words carried, once again reminded that we both stemmed from the same core, and perhaps Tynan's hatred of me was the same as my hatred for him. And if we shared the same hatred ...

"Then maybe we aren't so different after all. You can't remember anything either, can you?"

A shudder ran through my body.

Our thoughts had always *"… been distinct, but now they are blending, mixing with …"* one another, merging into a singular self.

"No! We are not the same! Nor will we ever be!"

"But until that ember is extinguished, I will haunt you. A reminder of an evil you cannot forget!"

"Get the fuck out of my head!"

"I can't, Raith … it's my head as much as it is yours. Anyway, I should let you wake up. The traitor and the whore will be getting worried about you."

Chapter 14
All Routes Lead to Home
2150 to 2152, Common Era – the Republic of Humanity

As I stood on the bridge of an Empire frigate, awaiting departure, I mused on the events of the last few days.

I'd started by bringing the U.E.R Council up to speed on what had transpired with the conversion device. It turned out that the Council and the Insurgency had worked together all along, jointly sabotaging the Empire in secret. As per Zavis's promises, the Council remained adamant about their expectations of me to carry on and convert all the Empire's worlds. After failing to negotiate an alternative, I'd reluctantly agreed – eventually seeing the logic of it – it was the path of least bloodshed after all. But it wasn't all give though: the Council had agreed to formally merge the Republic and the Empire into a new, joint government known as the Republic of Humanity, bringing support and ethical protection to the Empire's old worlds and sharing the Empire's private worlds and technologies with the new Republic.

Thus, acting as Tynan, I'd issued an Empire-wide communications blackout due to Insurgency infiltration and instructed them to await a personal visit from me before resuming connectivity.

I'd balked at the prospect of going into cryosleep again for the Empire's reformation tour, opting instead to experience the journey the slow way, and Amorina had volunteered to do the same to keep me company. The plan was to convert Terranova, then Astarte, Machina Station, Ares, then finally, Gaia, and the smaller moons along the way. The sun would set on the Empire's reign and rise again on a renewed humanity, free and united.

"Five minutes till departure, Raith," said the ship's captain, breaking me away from my thoughts.

"Thank you, Captain."

"Have you ever travelled the slow way before, Raith?"

"I have not."

"It's slow, obviously, but it has some exciting moments too! You'll see what I mean shortly, but first, you might want to take a seat," the captain said, motioning to an available seat.

"Thank you," I replied, taking up the offer.

"Flight control, we are ready to depart."

"Affirmative, Captain. Spooling warp engines now."

The ship began to vibrate, and a quiet hum filled the air.

"Engines spooled. Warping in three … two … one … warp!"

Outside the bridge's windows, I watched as every point of light in view shifted: first to blue, then to purple, only to then disappear altogether. Moments later, the entire view filled with a hazy blue hue before narrowing down to a blue cone, brightest at the centre and fading to black as it moved outward.

"Warp achieved."

"That was incredible!" I exclaimed. "But what did I just see?"

The captain chuckled. "You just witnessed the transition to warp. First, you saw visible light colour shifting into violet and then into ultraviolet wavelengths – becoming invisible to us, of course! Finally, the cosmic microwave background radiation, usually unperceivable, colour shifted into the visible spectrum, giving us the blue glow, which then warped around us, creating the cone effect that you can now see."

"What an amazing spectacle!"

❦

If there was one thing the slow form of space travel gave you, it was time. As we hurtled through space, there were no fields to plough, no soldiers to avoid, and no regimes to overthrow.

I'd find myself staring out the window of my quarters, watching the edge of the light cone fade into the perpetual darkness of space, overwhelmed and in awe of its vast, majestic beauty.

The skeleton crew, and the equally sparse facilities, provided minimal stimulation. Within the minimalist quarters, an inexhaustive collection of media, encompassing everything from nature documentaries to semi-recent blockbusters, was intended to be the solution to boredom.

With all of this in mind, I was highly grateful for Amorina's presence because I could only mindlessly watch so much media. Instead, when Amorina wasn't having time to herself, we would converse about life, the universe, and everything, and when we weren't talking, we would have sex ... lots of sex.

We would get lost in each other. Hours felt like minutes as we embraced one another, entwining mind, body, and soul. Each engagement allowed us to live out many lives. We became explorers, traversing wild and untamed lands, seeking pleasurable treasure; and we were dancers, leading and following, lost in the rhythm, slaves to the beat and its inevitable climax.

I closed my eyes and gave my head a shake, breaking away from the outside view. It was strange how the blue spectacle could capture and hold your attention whilst the world around you passed by. I turned my gaze instead to Amorina lying beside me. The quarters lighting was off presently, so the only illumination came from outside, bathing the room in a dim, eerie light.

In the darkness, it gave form to her body, barely visible like a sleeping ghost. She was resting on her side, her head rested upon her left arm and her hair tucked underneath it.

My eyes followed the highlighted edge of her body; travelling from her head up to the peak of her shoulder, before dropping down to the valley of her waist, only to rise up and over the rolling curve of her buttocks, dropping once more and following along her legs, which disappeared beneath the sheets.

As I watched, she shifted in her sleep, pulling the sheets up a little higher, adjusting her weight before settling down again. She uttered a faint mumble, and then her normal rhythmic breathing resumed. I wondered what thoughts were flickering through her mind, what dreamscapes her subconscious was exploring. Were they happy, or were they dreary? Were they bright, or were they dark? I hoped, of course, for the former scenarios, but I knew she'd experienced trauma these past days and knew how that could affect a person.

My dreams were still devoid and empty, with few long-term memories from which to construct elaborate places for my mind to inhabit in its sleep. The ember of Tynan still burned within, dragging me back to his dark beach, which, night after night, terrorised me with a horrifying thought: if Amorina weren't with me, I'd be alone, floating endlessly in the sea and in space – dark, cold, and lonely.

But I knew how to shine a light on the darkness. I would focus on my dream of living the good life: Amorina and I on a farm of our own, starting a family and working the land. We wouldn't have to worry about the rest of the universe – only each other and our children. That was the dream.

❈❈❈

The dropship hurtling through Terranova's atmosphere was a whole new experience for me. Every other planetary ascent and descent I'd experienced had been spent in cryosleep. This time I witnessed the terrifying beauty of atmospheric entry first-hand.

When the dropship had entered the atmosphere, a pale orange plasma had appeared around the outside of the ships' magnetic shielding, transforming into a dark red plasma as the descent progressed. The deceleration applied four g-forces to myself and the other occupants, which pressed me into my seat and made breathing difficult. As the ship passed into the troposphere, the in-atmosphere engines engaged, bringing the dropship under controlled flight.

"Another first for you, Raith. What did you think?" asked the pilot.

"Amazing! But also terrifying!"

"I know what you mean! The feeling never changes, even after hundreds of drops!"

I unbuckled myself from the seat, walking over to the back of the cabin and pulling the conversion device from its storage.

"We'll be touching down in a minute."

"Thanks, mate."

As I switched the device on, I could feel the dropship decelerating, swinging around as its landing spot was picked before touching down with a thud.

Now that we were on the ground, the hatch between the cockpit and the cargo bay opened, so I picked up the device and walked through. The rear cargo door was already opening, allowing fresh air and new light to stream into the ship. I inhaled, enjoying the new smells this alien air offered me. Adjusting to the light, I could see a welcome party of Empire officers waiting outside.

"Welcome, Your Grace, to Terranova. I am Commander Val."

"Thank you, Commander, for your welcome. It is good to be here."

"Yes, it's been a long time, hasn't it? I remember my father regaling tales of seeing you here as a child, having accompanied your father on one of his visits."

"Yes, it has been such a long time, so long in fact that I hardly remember coming here. Allow me a few minutes to take it all in."

"Of course, Your Grace."

I turned my back to the welcoming party, activating the conversion device. Immediately, its loud hum filled the air as it'd done previously.

"If I may inquire, Your Grace, what are you doing?"

"The device I hold is scanning the planet for conflicting ideals and dissidence. Let it do its work."

As the device hummed in my hands, I took in the beautiful Terranova landscape: rolling hills were covered in a sea of purple grass, broken up by the odd blue leafed trees. Nestled in the valleys were pools of crystal-clear water, several of which had people swimming in them, nude and carefree. True to its reputation, Terranova was a pleasure world, evidenced by a large orgy taking place in the distance. Dotted around the landscape, smaller groups and pairings could also be seen copulating. In a different life, I might've been captivated by such sights and rushed off to join in, but I knew the truth of this world: many of the workers here were the victims of Soul Harvests, plucked from their worlds.

The device was ready now, its hum dropping swiftly, shifting down into a bass rumble.

It cycled up and down, again and again, getting deeper and deeper, until its wave of energy burst forth, rushing out across the planet's surface.

In the sky above, numerous dropships appeared, carrying Republic troops who would assist in the planets' transition and rehabilitation.

❧❦❧

As the frigate dropped out of warp, it struck me how one and a half years is quite a long time to spend travelling through space. After Terranova's conversion, we'd made the short hop to Astarte, which had also been converted cleanly. From there, it was another six months to Machina Station. During the journey, Amorina had begun to feel ill in the mornings. Once we'd converted the station, we sought a doctor who confirmed our suspicions – we were expecting a child. Against the doctor's advice, we decided to keep Amorina out of cryosleep, and the doctor subsequently chose to accompany us for the continuation of our journey. Our daughter, Emma, was born on the way to Ares, becoming the first human born during warp travel. Gazing out the bridge windows, I looked down upon Ares – our final stop before we would finally be home.

"Captain … I'm picking up three frigates. They've just appeared from the other side of Ares, and they're heading towards us."

"Increase shield power to one hundred percent and try to open a communications channel."

As the pilot configured the shields, I turned to the Captain. "Can we withstand an attack from three frigates?"

"Not for long, but we just need to survive long enough for the Republic ships to get here."

"Captain, I've established a communication channel."

"The frigates three, this is Captain Mackenzie of the Empire Frigate Stormfalcon. Identify yourselves."

"Drop the pretence, Captain, the jig is up!" came the reply from a gruff and grizzled voice.

"There is no pretence here. I am carrying the emperor on board. So I repeat, this is Captain Mackenzie of the Empire Frigate Stormfalcon, identify yourselves."

"Listen, you fucking twat, I know what's been happening! The Emperor is a traitor to his Empire, and you lot have been going from world to world changing everybody. We will not be lambs to the slaughter like those other worlds. You want to change us? You'll have to do it to our dead bodies!"

The captain made a hand gesture to the pilot, who in turn pressed a button on the console.

"We're muted, Captain."

"How do you want to play this, Raith?"

"Let's try a little honesty. I suspect if we keep playing ignorant, we'll just aggravate them."

"Very well. Make us live, please."

The pilot pressed the console button again and then gave a thumbs up.

"Hi there … this is Raith speaking, formally known as Tynan Khidar."

"You fucking wanker! Do you know what you've done? How much work you've destroyed?"

"I don't see it as destruction, but rather transformation and rebirth."

"Of course you bloody well do … goddamn traitor!"

"May I know who I'm speaking with?"

"General Harry Jake is who's speaking! And I will have you know that I gave my life in service to the Empire. I served under your father, and subsequently under you, and helped build the Empire into what it was … until you started tearing it down. But I will not let you tear it down any further!"

"Captain, they've killed the channel … and they've fired missiles!"

"Fire countermeasures."

Watching closely, I spotted dozens of bullets streaking away from us, glinting as they reflected light from the system's star.

"Rail guns?" I asked.

"Yep!"

Ahead, I watched the bullets collide with the missiles, breaking chunks off its surface and altering their course. The missiles passed us by harmlessly, wobbling and twisting in an uncontrolled trajectory.

"Captain, they're changing tactic — they've deployed their rail guns."

"Prepare for evasive manoeuvres!"

Suddenly, out of the corner of my eye, a large object appeared, catching the star's light as it shot across my field of view. The projectile punched through the middle of the leftmost frigate, tearing it in half.

"Ah!" the captain exclaimed. "The cavalry has arrived!"

I looked out the window to see a Republic Cruiser and two accompanying frigates.

"You're lucky your friends showed up, Raith! Just know this fight isn't over!"

The short message from the General filled the bridge as his two remaining ships quickly rotated and began accelerating away.

"Intrepid is charging its Gauss Cannon again! We'll get them!"

"Can you open a channel to the Intrepid, please?"

"Sure thing," said the pilot, giving me a thumbs-up.

"Intrepid, this is Raith on the Stormfalcon."

"Howdy, Raith. How you doin'?"

"I am doing very well, thanks to you! A quick request though — please don't shoot down those frigates."

"Can do, but they'll return and be problematic when they do ... so may I ask why?"

"Maybe they will be back, and maybe they will be a problem ... but maybe they'll also remember the mercy they were shown."

"Very well then, if you're sure, sir."

"Thank you! We'll be commencing planetfall shortly."

"Acknowledged. Good luck to you. Intrepid out."

In the distance, I watched both frigates blip away as they warped off to an unknown destination.

"Won't they be a problem at some point?" the captain asked.

"Possibly, but we will tackle it if it becomes a problem. For now, we've got a job to do."

❈❈❈

The dropship docked back with the frigate, another conversion successfully behind me. As its hanger door opened, Amorina was standing there waiting for me, gently cradling Emma in her arms.

"Hey you," she said with a smile. "Mission go well?"

"Yes, it seemed the General had tried to gather support, but most of the soldiers believed the emperor incorruptible. So we were welcomed on arrival and converted them easily."

"I'm glad to hear it. Does that mean we can go home now?"

"Yes ... yes, it does!"

"I can't wait to see our parents and have them meet Emma."

"Eight months will pass before you know it, and we won't have to leave home again."

"That's the bit I'm looking forward to most ... I think I've just about had enough of space travel."

"I know, me too."

Chapter 15
An Evil ... Forgotten?

2152, Common Era – Planet Gaia, Outer Rim, Republic of Humanity

The arrival of a stranger was hardly ever a good thing, particularly on Gaia. When ships fell from the sky, it was the arrival of either the Empire or pirates. As our dropship descended, I could only imagine the fear that was beginning to stir in the people below. Then I imagined confusion entering their thoughts as they recognised an Empire dropship dropping from the sky. And if it was a Soul Harvest, it was happening a year too early and with a few dozen ships too few.

"Could you land us in the town centre, please?"

The pilot glanced out the window.

"It'll be a bit tight, but I should be able to make it happen!"

The ship slowed down, circled as it got closer to its landing site. I looked out the cockpit window and saw my parents and Amorina's mother present in the crowd below. Butterflies flurried in my stomach as I thought about being with them again. I listened to the hum of the engines and the way their sound changed as the ship landed: growing louder as it decelerated the vessel, controlling its descent to touchdown; softening as the engines cycled down once landfall had been made.

"Are you ready?" I asked, turning to Amorina.

"I'm so ready!"

I opened the hatch to the cargo bay, and we both inhaled the rush of air flowing in through the open rear cargo door.

"Fuck me, that smells so good!" Amorina explained.

"It smells like home!"

"Yes, it does. Shall we set foot on our home soil?"

"Absolutely!"

"Well, after you …"

I walked through the hatch, across the length of the cargo bay and then out into the open. Transitioning from the dark interior of the dropship to the bright streets of Gaia overwhelmed my eyes, and for a few moments, I was blind. My ears were met with almost complete silence. At first, I could hear only the shuffling of feet – people moving around to try and get a better view of the new arrival. As human-shaped blobs began to register with my eyes, whispers started to trickle into my ears. My surroundings became more apparent as clothing and faces became distinguishable.

"Raith?" a quiet and familiar voice spoke above the whispers.

I turned towards the sound, scanning the faces for the face I knew to be there.

"Raith? Is it really you?"

There I saw her, my mother. I smiled, and moments later, I watched her face break out into a huge grin as well.

"Oh, Raith! It is you! It is you!" she squealed, running forward to embrace me.

As I held her in my arms, I looked back out at the crowd and spotted my father. A small smile crept onto his face, and he began to walk towards me. As if sensing his presence, my mother let go of me and stepped back, allowing my father through.

"Son … how are you?" he said quietly.

"I picked a wolf … and I came home."

The smile on my father's face grew, and his eyes moistened. "I'm thrilled to hear that."

He stepped forward at last and embraced me.

"Raith?" another voice called out.

My father let me go, and I turned to find Amorina's mother coming towards me. Her face was scarred and bent, a painful reminder of the sacrifice she'd provided to get me off-world.

"Raith … did you find her? Did you save Amorina?"

"Hi, Anne. Yes, I did. She's on the ship."

Anne nodded and turned towards the ship, where Amorina was just emerging from the darkness. Anne started to rush forwards and then stopped, having spotted the bundle in Amorina's arms.

"Mother, Father … Anne, I'd like you to meet Emma … your granddaughter."

Both Mother and Anne simultaneously let out high pitched squeaks and then rushed forward to greet Amorina and swoon over the baby in her arms.

I turned to look back at my father.

"You didn't come home alone then," he said.

"No. I came back with so much more. An understanding of who I was, who I am, and who I want to be. As it turned out, this wasn't my first family, but I wasn't a good father or a good man beforehand. I intend to do better this time and right the wrongs of the past, so there's a few people on ice in the ship that I'm keen for you to get to know as well."

"I look forward to it … over a celebratory dinner, perhaps?"

"That sounds wonderful!"

"Great! Come on, let's get started – the ladies will be distracted for a while, methinks."

"Definitely! But I have one thing to do first."

I turned towards the ship and made a hand gesture to come closer. The pilot appeared from within the ship, carrying the conversion device.

As he handed it over, primed and ready, I rested my thumbs on the triggers.

"What is that?"

"Peace and unity."

I pressed the triggers, and the device began its charging sequence.

"Soon, the Empire will be all but a memory of the past ... and all of its wrongdoing and dark deeds can be consigned to history ... perhaps one day becoming nothing more than a forgotten evil."

"That device is going to do all that?"

"Yep."

"How?"

"By changing people and their thoughts, modifying their ideals."

"And the people ... they've no choice in the matter?"

"Father, believe me, I argued this point too. It seemed just as bad as the villainy I was trying to erase ... but trust me, it was the only way to ensure the right wolf won."

My father nodded, processing what he'd just heard. I had sometimes wondered if my father had had his suspicions about who I really was. I'd thought that perhaps that's why he'd championed so hard, fighting to teach me that who I was, was a choice. Now I knew he'd been right, that power always had been mine, but it was his guidance that allowed me to see it, and in the end choose who I wanted to be.

"I know I'm taking away people's choices ... but there was no other way."

❈

Shortly after the conversion, the Republic's forces landed, supporting the converted and beginning construction of an outpost that would link us to the core worlds, supporting the new government.

I'd woken up my son, my two daughters, and their mothers from cryosleep. I introduced them to the rest of the community when they came together for the celebrations. We constructed a large bonfire, and as the day grew long and the size of the fire diminished, we roasted a meal over its glowing coals. After we'd eaten, I regaled my adventures to the crowds.

I spoke of space stations and insurgencies, and I recalled worlds of war and planets of pleasure. I told them of Earth and Mars, the homes of our ancestors and how they differed from our frontier. But I also shared with them the truth of who I'd been. That the emperor had lived among them, unknown even to himself, and how a journey to the stars had revealed the truth to the man he'd become. I told them how I'd been tempted by lust and power into becoming that man again but that the life I'd lived here, and the people I'd met along the way, had swayed me from treading down that dark path.

After that, they briefly shared their own stories: how four years had passed quickly for them, as most years did. They spoke of how their thoughts had often turned to me, thinking of my journey amongst the stars, wondering if the man who'd stood up to the Empire had been successful in chasing after the women he loved. They'd often pondered over my fate: had I survived or had I died, had I found Amorina or not?

And now they knew: not only had Amorina and I survived, but I'd brought the Empire to its knees.

"Thank you, Raith, for all you've done! You've given us a freedom we never thought possible."

The crowd murmured their agreement with the statement.

"But before we let you rest, what is the plan for the future? Who controls all the power?"

I waited for a moment, collecting my thoughts as the crowd watched, waiting for a response.

"This place where we find ourselves, of a humanity united, that is the future. I worked with the United Earth

Republic; I discussed a transition of power to ensure that a dissolved Empire wouldn't fall into despair and ruin. They agreed, and together we formed the Republic of Humanity, a democratic entity to rule fairly over the human domain. They control the power now." I paused, watching their faces, judging their reactions.

"The United Earth Republic had its fair share of dark history – more wars than I can count, just on Earth alone, never mind the Martian war before unification. They've learned from their history, which is why they've become the republic they are and how they've stayed as one. The Empire provided another lesson: what happens when the darker elements of humanity are allowed to run amok across multiple worlds. That history provides a foundational lesson for the new republic." I paused again, allowing the crowd to utter an approving murmur.

"Humanity will continue to explore and expand, as it always has. Technological improvements will allow us to fly further and faster, spreading further into the stars. We don't know what lies out there, but whatever we find, or whatever finds us, we will face it together." I looked over at Amorina and my four children. "But more importantly, we will thrive together, free and united!"

The crowd cheered, and sensing that my speech was over, they returned to talking amongst themselves. I was about to head off when I saw my father wondering over.

"This has been really wonderful, son."

"Yes, it has been. Listen, I have something else to tell, and ah … well, it's probably going to ruin the mood, but I think you need to hear it."

"Is it about Livietta?"

"Yeah …"

"I already know. It's your mother that doesn't. But I keep it from her … it's easier for her to process, thinking that our daughter was taken and simply didn't come back."

"I … I see. How did you find out?"

"The Insurgency can do all sorts of things," my father replied, patting me on the back and walking away.

Yeah, that they can, I thought.

Wait a minute. The gravity of what my father had just said began to sink in. Hold the fuck up, I thought, does that mean … all this time … oh my fucking god – it does too!

⦑\⟨∨⟩⫽⦒

"That was a rousing speech you gave earlier."

I opened my eyes to find my sleep disrupted yet again, once more teleported into the depths of my subconscious.

"Tynan …" I growled.

"What I want to know is, can you thrive, free and united, when you are still divided?"

"Of course not … because you keep disturbing me at night."

"So why haven't you gotten rid of me?"

"I needed to complete the mission first."

"Have you completed the mission?"

"Yes …"

"Then why haven't you gotten rid of me?"

"I'm getting there, okay? Will you please shut the fuck up and let me sleep?"

"Did you ever consider what it's like for me, Raith?"

"What do you mean?"

"I am stuck in your head. I can't sleep. I can't dream. My existence is a literal endless, waking nightmare. I can't hide from it; I can't run from it; I can't escape my fate, not by my own hand."

"I … I didn't realise it was that bad for you."

"Well, it is! I've accepted that you've won. I told you I would haunt you, but I've had enough. Whatever sanity I had left, I can feel it slipping away from me … I'm going crazy in here!"

"So you want me to end you? … To snuff you out?"

"Yes! Do it! Extinguish my ember and allow me peace in my defeat!"

"Okay … let me wake up, and I'll finish this … for both of us."

"Thank you, Raith …"

❨❨❨❨

The spade bit into the ground and allowed me to scoop the last of the dirt from the hole. I deposited the soil onto a heap of excavated earth and then leaned the spade against a tree, stepping back and admiring my handiwork. I reached into my pocket and pulled out two holochips: the MIND AIs', both version one and two.

I threw them into the hole. Reaching into a different pocket, I pulled out a third holochip, upon which was scrawled "MAI 1.1". Back on Earth, I'd spoken to Zavis and explained that Tynan was still in my head after the Earth conversion. Zavis hypothesised that the standard conversion would be unable to remove the last of my dark side.

Before leaving, he'd handed me the modified AI and shown me how to configure the conversion device to affect a smaller radius. It was untested, but he was pretty sure it would work.

"Here goes nothing."

I picked up the conversion device, pressing the holochip into the slot. After a few setting changes, it was configured for a two hundred metre radius. As I rested my thumbs on the triggers, I felt a twinge of guilt. Not that I thought the AI was sentient or anything, but I wondered how it felt to be cast into a hole, entombed and forgotten.

"It's not your fault, you know," I said to the device as if it could hear me. "Your fate is just a consequence of your capability, rather than because of what you are, which objectively, is neither good nor evil. But your propensity to be used for harm is too great." I pressed down on the triggers and then lowered the device into the hole. "Because of that capability, you must never fall into the wrong hands or be unintentionally found. So, you will do what you do one more time. Bitsy will know where you lie, but I will not. You need to become a forgotten evil."

I quickly grabbed the shovel and moved the excavated soil back into the hole, burying the device and the chips. Once the hole was filled, I stomped on it, compacting the soil. Finally, I raised my wrist. "Bitsy, please save our current coordinates under the remembrance protocol."

Coordinates saved with the requested protocol.

From beneath my feet, I heard the first tonal drop from the device – its conversion blast was imminent, which meant it was time to go. I turned on the spot and ran, counting my paces as I sprinted, ensuring I didn't move outside the two hundred metre radius.

At about one hundred and fifty metres, I stopped just as I heard the device trigger. Turning around, I watched as the wave of energy moved towards me.

"Tynan ... I bid you farewell!"

I closed my eyes and spread my arms out wide, welcoming the energy wave as it embraced me.

❦

I awoke to water lapping at my face. Slowly I raised my heavy, aching head and looked around. I was lying at the edge of a river, the morning light gently filtering through the surrounding forest. Beside me lay a dirty shovel, but I could not recall if it was mine, and if it was, why I had it, or for what it had been used. Raising myself into a kneeling position, I saw my reflection in the water. I was a man, possibly in my late thirties: a receding hairline revealed a scar that encircled my head, running across my forehead. As I stared at my image, I realised I didn't know who I was, where I was, or why I was here. Then like a bubble rising to the surface, a name popped into my head: Raith.

Yes, that sounded familiar.

I was Raith.

I waited a bit longer, and more thoughts began to surface.

I was on the planet Gaia. I had four children and a partner. Her name was … Am … Amor … Amorina! Her name was Amorina.

I sat back, confident that my amnesia would pass and that I was who I was supposed to be and where I was supposed to be. Everything else … well, that would all work out in time, surely.

Epilogue
Something Wicked This Way Comes

2154, Common Era – Space, Beyond the Outer Rim

All signals travel, such is their nature, and the conversion device's Theta waves were no exception. From the early proof of concept tests carried out by the advisors, to the thirty times Raith had wielded its power; each time its signals had gone beyond its intended target, travelling further than the devices effective range. They travelled from the inner rim to the outer and beyond, slowly but surely traversing the vast dark expanses of space. Their journey took them past stars and planets, through asteroid fields and around gas giants, until they finally reached a dark and foreboding region.

Here, only death could be found. The signals passed through a graveyard of starships. Seven of them were humanities – the exploration vessels the Empire had sent out chasing the alien signal. But the thousands of other carcasses belonged to many a race, far older than humanity but dead nonetheless. Whatever prowess they might've claimed to have had possession over, here that power was relinquished. Now only their bones and creations could tell their stories, but there was no one here to read them.

If there was, they would've spoken of the many battles that'd taken place here; how race after race had fought, sacrificing their lives to stop the force which slumbered at the centre of this graveyard. It would've told tales of each ship and its crew; how fiercely they'd waged war against their foe, knowing they'd never make it home but fighting on anyway in the hopes that their homes would survive their demise. The ships too, would regale how they had fought and fallen, torn apart by their mighty adversary.

But alas, Theta signals couldn't read such stories from the dead, much less understand them.

Instead, they travelled further, right into the heart of this floating cemetery. The signals came across a great structure, passing through its external skin and into the structures within. The systems awakened as the Theta waves passed through its cold, empty halls and sleeping machinery. The presence of the signals triggered the slumbering menace, calling it to action. Its sensors awoke, detecting the signals. Its vast network of computing power began triangulating the signal's origin, plotting a course that it could follow once its mighty engines had fired up for the first time in many millennia.

This great construct was complex in many ways, simple in others. Its objectives were clear. Detect Theta waves. Find the source and destroy it. It had these objectives because it understood that in this galaxy, at least, Theta waves meant life. And it had been told long ago that life was the enemy. With those simple rules in mind, it had wielded great power against many a helpless victim. But its power was neither good nor evil; that distinction belonged to those who had created it and told it what the world was. But if the bones that now surround it could tell you what they saw it as, they would speak a clear and resounding answer: Forgotten Evil.

The Forgotten Saga Continues ...

Visit books2read.com/AwakenedHorror

Sign Up for Quill's Newsletter

Join Quill Holland's mailing list today, and you'll get not one but two free eBooks direct to your inbox!

Be among the first to learn about Quill's new releases & receive exclusive content, including sneak peeks, discounts, and giveaways! You'll be emailed once or twice a month, and you can unsubscribe anytime.

Sign up at www.quillholland.nz

Acknowledgements

A huge thank you to my alpha reader, Jonathan, whose contributions were essential as the story took shape, and to my beta readers, Ashley, Rachael, and Kevin, for helping to polish off the completed draft.

Thank you to my fantastic editor, Cherie, for all her proofing and editing work, and for making sure I wasn't too prolific with my ellipses.

A big shout out to Dewi Hargreaves for creating the marvellous map at the start of the book – thank you for bringing the interstellar world of Forgotten Evil to life!

Finally, a big thank you to my cover designer, David from Cover Creator, for his patience and perseverance, in bringing my cover to life during a pandemic.

Also by Quill Holland

The Forgotten Saga

Book 1: Forgotten Evil
Book 2: Awakened Horror

Short Stories

The Last of Her Kind
What Mattered Most

Pilgrimage of the Amalgamal
As featured in Lost Boys Press's 2023 Anthology,
Empire of Beasts

About the Author

A programmer by day and a writer by night, Quill Holland is a young New Zealand author who is always creating content. Ever since he was young, Quill could be found with his nose in a book or watching the latest science-fiction movie. As a result, he's developed an imagination that never stops, and naturally, sci-fi and fantasy are the domains that Quill's work inhabits.

A creative writing graduate from the New Zealand Institute of Business Studies and a member of the New Zealand Society of Authors, Quill has several self-published stories. When he's not debugging code or creating worlds, Quill likes to dabble in illustration and photography, as well as exploring the natural beauty of New Zealand with his partner.

Connect with Quill on:

Website: www.quillholland.nz
Twitter: @quill_holland
Facebook: @QuillHolland
Instagram: @quillholland
Goodreads: @quillholland